The Secret of the Old Clock

"The Crowley clock at last!" Nancy exclaimed

The Secret of the Old Clock

BY CAROLYN KEENE

GROSSET & DUNLAP
Publishers • New York
A member of The Putnam & Grosset Group

PRINTED ON RECYCLED PAPER

Contents

CHAPTER		PAGE
I	THE RESCUE	1
II	A MISSING WILL	11
III	AN UNPLEASANT MEETING	20
IV	RACING THE STORM	30
V	A SURPRISING STORY	39
VI	AN EXCITING APPOINTMENT	47
VII	THE ANGRY DOG	59
VIII	A FORGOTTEN SECRET	69
IX	HELPFUL DISCLOSURES	78
X	FOLLOWING A CLUE	88
XI	AN UNEXPECTED ADVENTURE	96
XII	A DESPERATE SITUATION	105
XIII	THE FRUSTRATING WAIT	111
XIV	A TENSE CHASE	119
XV	NANCY'S RISKY UNDERTAKING	127
XVI	THE CAPTURE	136
XVII	STRANGE INSTRUCTIONS	144
XVIII	A SUSPENSEFUL SEARCH	153
XIX	STARTLING REVELATIONS	163
XX	A HAPPY FINALE	171

The Secret of the Old Clock

CHAPTER I

The Rescue

NANCY DREW, an attractive girl of eighteen, was driving home along a country road in her new, dark-blue convertible. She had just delivered some legal papers for her father.

"It was sweet of Dad to give me this car for my birthday," she thought. "And it's fun to help him in his work."

Her father, Carson Drew, a well-known lawyer in their home town of River Heights, frequently discussed puzzling aspects of cases with his blond, blue-eyed daughter.

Smiling, Nancy said to herself, "Dad depends on my intuition."

An instant later she gasped in horror. From the lawn of a house just ahead of her a little girl about five years of age had darted into the roadway. A van, turning out of the driveway of the house, was barely fifty feet away from her. As the driver vigorously sounded the horn in warning, the child became confused and ran directly in front of the van. Miraculously, the little girl managed to cross the road safely and pull herself up onto a low wall, which formed one side of a bridge. But the next second, as the van sped away, the child lost her balance and toppled off the wall out of sight!

"Oh my goodness!" Nancy cried out, slamming on her brakes. She had visions of the child plunging into the water below, perhaps striking her head fatally on a rock!

Nancy leaped out of her car and dashed across the road. At the foot of the embankment, she could see the curly-haired little girl lying motionless, the right side of her body in the water.

"I hope—" Nancy dared not complete the harrowing thought as she climbed down the steep slope.

When she reached the child, she saw to her great relief that the little girl was breathing normally and no water had entered her nose or mouth. A quick examination showed that she had suffered no broken bones.

Gently Nancy lifted the little girl, and holding her firmly in both arms, struggled to the top of the embankment. Then she hurried across the road and up the driveway to the child's house.

At this moment the front door flew open and an elderly woman rushed out, crying, "Judy! Judy!"

The next second, the child lost her balance

"I'm sure she'll be all right," said Nancy quickly.

The woman, seeing Nancy's car, asked excitedly, "Did you run into her?"

"No, no. Judy fell off the bridge." Nancy quickly explained what had taken place.

By this time another woman, slightly younger, had hurried from the house. "Our baby! What has happened to her?"

As the woman reached out to take Judy, Nancy said soothingly, "Judy's going to be all right. I'll carry her into the house and lay her on a couch."

One of the women opened the screen door and the other directed, "This way."

Nancy carried her little burden through a hallway and into a small, old-fashioned living room. As soon as she laid the child on the couch, Judy began to murmur and turn her head from side to side.

"I believe she'll come to in a few minutes," said Nancy.

The two women watched Judy intently as they introduced themselves as Edna and Mary Turner, great-aunts of the little girl.

"Judy lives with us," explained Edna, the older sister. "We're bringing her up."

Nancy was somewhat surprised to hear that these elderly women were rearing such a small child. She gave her name and address, just as Judy opened her eyes and looked around. Seeing Nancy, she asked, "Who are you?"

"My name is Nancy. I'm glad to know you, Judy."

"Did you see me fall?"

Nancy nodded, as the child's Aunt Mary said, "She rescued you from the river after you fell in."

Judy began to cry. "I'll never, never run into the road again, really I won't!" she told her aunts.

Nancy said she was sure that Judy never would. She patted the child, who smiled up at her. Although Nancy felt that Judy would be all right, she decided to stay a few minutes longer to see if she could be of help. The child's wet clothes were removed and a robe put on her.

Mary Turner started for the kitchen door. "I'd better get some medication and wet compresses for Judy. She's getting a good-sized lump on her head. Nancy, will you come with me?"

She led the way to the kitchen and headed for a first-aid cabinet which hung on the wall.

"I want to apologize to you, Nancy, for thinking you hit Judy," the woman said. "I guess Edna and I lost our heads. You see, Judy is very precious to us. We brought up her mother, who had been an only child and was orphaned when she was a little girl. The same thing happened to Judy. Her parents were killed in a boat explosion three years ago. The poor little girl has no close relatives except Edna and me."

"Judy looks very healthy and happy," Nancy said quickly, "so I'm sure she must love it here."

Mary smiled. "We do the best we can on our small income. Sometimes it just doesn't suffice, though. We sold some old furniture to the two men in that van you saw. I don't know who they were, but I guess the price was all right."

Mary Turner's thoughts went back to little Judy. "She's so little now that Edna and I are able to manage with our small income. But we worry about the future. We're dressmakers but our fingers aren't so nimble with the needle as they used to be.

"To tell you the truth, Nancy, at the time Judy's parents were killed, Edna and I wondered whether we would be able to take care of Judy properly. But we decided to try it and now we wouldn't part with her for anything in the world. She's won our hearts completely."

Nancy was touched by the story. She knew what was in the minds of the Turner sisters—living costs would become higher, and with their advancing years, their own income would become lower.

"Unfortunately," Mary went on, "Judy's parents left very little money. But they were extremely bright people and Judy is going to be like them. She ought to study music and dancing, and have a college education. But I'm afraid we'll never be able to give her those things."

Nancy said reassuringly, "Judy may be able to win a scholarship, or get other financial aid."

Mary, finding Nancy a sympathetic listener, continued, "A cousin of our father's named Josiah Crowley used to help us. But he passed away a couple of months ago. For years he used to pay us long visits and was very generous with his money." Miss Turner sighed. "He always promised to remember us in his will—he loved little Judy—and I am afraid Edna and I came to depend on that in our plans for her. But he did not carry out his promise."

Nancy smiled understandingly and made. no comment. But she did wonder why Mr. Crowley had changed his mind.

"Josiah went to live with some other cousins. After that, things changed. He rarely came to see us. But he was here just last February and said the same thing—that Edna and I were to inherit money from him. He had always helped us and it seemed strange that he should stop so suddenly."

Mary Turner looked at Nancy. "Maybe you know our well-to-do cousins that he went to stay with. They live in River Heights. They're the Richard Tophams."

"Do they have two daughters named Ada and Isabel?" Nancy asked. "If so, I know them."

"That's the family all right," replied Mary.

Nancy detected a hint of coolness in the woman's voice. "Do you like those two girls?" Miss Turner asked.

Nancy did not answer at once. She had been taught never to gossip. But finally she said tactfully, "Ada and Isabel were in high school with me. They were never my close friends. We—uh —didn't see eye to eye on various things."

By this time Mary Turner had selected a few items from the first-aid chest. Now she went to the refrigerator for some ice cubes. As she arranged the various articles on a tray, she said, "Well, when Cousin Josiah passed away, to our amazement Richard Topham produced a will which made him executor of the Crowley estate and left all the money to him, his wife, and the two girls."

"Yes. I did read that in the newspaper," Nancy recalled. "Is the estate a large one?"

"I understand there's considerable money in it," Mary Turner replied. "Some of Josiah's other cousins say he told them the same thing he told us, and they are planning to go to court about the matter." The woman shrugged. "But I guess a fight to break the will would be hopeless. Nevertheless, Edna and I cannot help feeling there *must* be a later will, although as yet no one has presented it."

Nancy followed Miss Turner into the living room. The cold compresses helped to reduce the swelling where Judy had hit her head on a rock. Convinced now that the little girl was all right, Nancy said she must leave.

"Come to see me again soon," Judy spoke up. "I like you, Nancy. "You're my saving girl."

"You bet I'll come," Nancy answered. "I like you too. You're a good sport!"

The child's great-aunts profusely thanked Nancy again for rescuing Judy. The visitor had barely reached the door when Edna suddenly said, "Mary, where's our silver teapot?"

"Why, right there on the tea table— Oh, it's gone!"

Edna ran into the dining room. "The silver candlesticks! They're gone too!"

Nancy had paused in the doorway, startled. "Do you mean the pieces have been stolen?" she asked.

"They must have been," replied Mary Turner, who was white with apprehension. "By those men who bought some furniture from us!"

Instantly Nancy thought of the men in the van. "Who were the men?" she asked.

"Oh, Mary, how could we have been so careless?" Edna Turner wailed. "We don't know who the men were. They just knocked on the door and asked if we had any old furniture that we wanted to sell. We'll never get the silver back!"

"Maybe you will!" said Nancy. "I'll call the police."

"Oh dear!" Mary said woefully. "Our phone is out of order."

"Then I'll try to catch up to the van!" Nancy declared. "What did the men look like?"

"They were short and heavy-set. One had dark hair, the other light. They had kind of large noses. That's about all I noticed."

"Me too," said Edna.

With a hasty good-by Nancy dashed from the house and ran to her car.

CHAPTER II

A Missing Will

THE BLUE convertible sped along the country road. Nancy smiled grimly.

"I'm afraid I'm exceeding the speed limit," she thought. "But I almost wish a trooper would stop me. Then I could tell him what happened to the poor Turner sisters."

Nancy watched the tire marks which the van driven by the thieves had evidently made in the dirt road. But a few miles farther on a feeling of dismay came over her. She had reached a V-shaped intersection of two highways. Both roads were paved, and since no tire impressions could be seen, Nancy did not know which highway the thieves had taken.

"Oh dear!" she sighed. "Now what shall I do?"

Nancy concluded that her wisest move would be to take the road which led to River Heights. There was a State Police barracks just a few miles ahead.

"I'll stop there and report the theft."

She kept looking for the van, which she recalled as charcoal gray. "I wish I'd seen the license number or the name of the firm that owns the van," Nancy said to herself ruefully.

When she reached State Police headquarters Nancy introduced herself to Captain Runcie and told about the robbery, giving what meager information she could about the suspects. The officer promised to send out an alarm immediately for the thieves and their charcoal-gray moving van.

Nancy continued her journey home, thinking of the Turners and their problems.

"I wonder why Mr. Josiah Crowley left all his money to the Tophams and none to his other relatives. Why did he change his mind? Those Tophams are well to do and don't need money as much as the Turners."

Nancy did not know Richard Topham, but she was acquainted with his wife, as well as his daughters. They were arrogant and unreasonable, and disliked by many of the shopkeepers in town. Ada and Isabel had been unpopular in high school. They had talked incessantly of money and social position, making themselves very obnoxious to the other students.

"I wonder," Nancy thought, "if a way can't be found so the Turners could get a share of the Crowley money. I'll ask Dad."

Five minutes later Nancy pulled into the double

garage and hurried across the lawn to the kitchen door of the Drews' large red-brick house. The building stood well back from the street, and was surrounded by tall, beautiful trees.

"Hello, Nancy," greeted the pleasant, slightly plump woman who opened the door. She was Hannah Gruen, housekeeper for the Drews, who had helped rear Nancy since the death of the girl's own mother many years before.

Nancy gave her a hug, then asked, "Dad home? I see his car is in the garage."

"Your father's in the living room and dinner will be ready in a few minutes."

Nancy went to say hello to her tall, handsome father, then hurried to wash her hands and comb her hair before the three who formed the Drew household sat down to dinner. During the meal Nancy related her adventure of the afternoon.

"What tricky thieves!" Hannah Gruen burst out. "Oh, I hope the police capture them!"

"They certainly took advantage of those Turner sisters," Mr. Drew commented.

"Mary and Edna are in financial difficulties," Nancy commented. "Isn't it a shame that Josiah Crowley didn't bequeath some of his estate to the Turners and other relatives who need the money?"

Carson Drew smiled affectionately at his only child, then said, "Yes, it is, Nancy. But unless a will written later turns up, that's the way it has to be."

"The Turners think there is another will," Nancy told him. "Wouldn't it be wonderful if it can be found?"

"I agree," spoke up Hannah. "It's well known in town that Mrs. Topham and her daughters were unkind to Josiah Crowley for some time before he died. Their excuse was that Josiah's eccentricities were extremely trying."

"The Tophams have never been noted for any charitable inclinations," Mr. Drew observed with a smile. "However, they did give Josiah a home."

"Only because they knew he was going to leave all his money to them," said Hannah. "If I'd been Josiah I wouldn't have stayed there." The housekeeper sighed. "But when people get old, they don't like change. And probably he put up with things rather than move."

She said the treatment the Tophams had accorded old Josiah Crowley had aroused a great deal of unfavorable comment throughout River Heights. Nancy had not known him personally, but she had often seen the elderly man on the street. Secretly she had regarded him as a rather nice, kindly person.

His wife had died during an influenza epidemic and after that he had made his home with various relatives. According to rumors, all these people had admitted that he had paid his board and done many favors for them. They in turn had been very kind to him, and though poor themselves, had tried to make Josiah Crowley comfortable and happy.

"Tell me everything you know about Mr. Crowley," Nancy urged her father.

The lawyer said that the old man had publicly declared he intended to provide in his will for several deserving relatives and friends. Then, three years before his death, the Topham family, who had never shown an interest in him, had experienced a sudden change of heart. They had begged Josiah Crowley to make his home with them, and at last he had consented. Shortly after he moved into the Topham house, Mr. Drew was told that the old man had decided to leave all his money to them.

Mr. Crowley, though failing in health, maintained a firm grip on life. But as time went on, he became more and more unhappy. He continued to live with the Tophams, but it was whispered about that he frequently slipped away to visit his other relatives and friends, and that he intended to change his will again.

"Then there must be a later will!" Nancy said hopefully.

Mr. Drew nodded, and went on, "One day Josiah Crowley became critically ill. Just before his death he attempted to communicate something to the doctor who attended him, but his words, other than 'will,' were unintelligible. After the funeral only one will came to light, giving the entire fortune to the Tophams."

"Dad, do you suppose Mr. Crowley was trying to tell the doctor something about another will which he had put some place where the Tophams couldn't find it?" Nancy asked.

"Very likely," the lawyer replied. "Probably he intended to leave his money to relatives who had been kind to him. But fate cheated him of the opportunity."

"Do you think anybody has looked for another will?" Nancy questioned.

"I don't know. But I'm sure of this. If another will shows up, Richard Topham will fight it. The estate is a considerable one, I understand, and they aren't the kind of people to share good fortune."

"Can't the present will be contested?" Nancy asked.

"I hear that other relatives have filed a claim, declaring they were told another will had been made in their favor. But unless it is located, I doubt that the matter will ever go further."

"But the Tophams don't deserve the fortune," Hannah Gruen remarked. "And besides, they don't need the money. It doesn't seem fair."

"It may not seem fair, but it is legal," Mr. Drew told her, "and I'm afraid nothing can be done about the situation."

"Poor Judy and her aunts!" said Nancy.

"There are others affected in the same way," her father remarked. "For instance, two young women who live on the River Road. I don't know their names. I understand they were not related to Mr. Crowley, but were great favorites of his. They are having a struggle and could use some extra money."

Nancy lapsed into silence. She felt strongly that a mystery lurked behind the Crowley case.

"Dad, don't *you* believe Josiah Crowley made a second will?" Nancy questioned suddenly.

"You sound like a trial lawyer, the way you cross-examine me," Mr. Drew protested, but with evident enjoyment. "To tell the truth, Nancy, I don't know what to think, but something did happen which might indicate that Mr. Crowley at least intended to make another will."

"Please go on!" Nancy begged impatiently.

"Well, one day nearly a year ago I was in the First National Bank when Crowley came in with Henry Rolsted."

"The attorney who specializes in wills and other estate matters?" Nancy inquired.

"Yes. I had no intention of listening to their conversation, but I couldn't help overhearing a few words that made me think they were discussing a will. Crowley made an appointment to call at Rolsted's office the following day."

"Oh!" cried Nancy excitedly. "That looks as though Mr. Crowley had made a new will, doesn't it? But why didn't Mr. Rolsted say something about it at the time of Mr. Crowley's death?"

"For one of many reasons," Mr. Drew replied. "In the first place, he may never have drawn a new will for Mr. Crowley. And even if he had, the old man might have changed his mind again and torn it up."

Before Nancy spoke again, she finished the delicious apple pudding which Hannah had made. Then she looked thoughtfully at her father. "Dad, Mr. Rolsted is an old friend of yours, isn't he?"

"Yes. An old friend and college classmate."

"Then won't you please ask him if he ever drew up a will for Mr. Crowley, or knows anything that might solve this mystery?"

"That's a rather delicate question, young lady. He may tell me it's none of my business!"

"You know he won't. You're such good friends he'll understand why you're taking a special interest in this case. Will you do it? Please!"

"I know you like to help people who are in trouble," her father said. "I suppose I could invite Mr. Rolsted to have lunch with me tomorrow—"

"Wonderful!" Nancy interrupted eagerly. "That would be a splendid opportunity to find out what he knows about a later will."

"All right. I'll try to arrange a date. How about joining us?"

Nancy's face lighted up as she said, "Oh, thank you, Dad. I'd love to. I hope it can be tomorrow, so we won't have to waste any time trying to find another will."

Mr. Drew smiled. "We?" he said. "You mean you might try to find a hidden will if Mr. Crowley wrote one?"

"I might." Nancy's eyes sparkled in anticipation.

CHAPTER III

An Unpleasant Meeting

"WHAT are your plans for this morning, Nancy?" her father asked at the breakfast table.

"I thought I'd do a little shopping," she replied. Her eyes twinkled. "There's a dance coming up at the country club and I'd like to get a new dress."

"Then will you phone me about lunch? Or better still, how about eating with me, whether Mr. Rolsted comes or not?"

"I'll be there!" Nancy declared gaily.

"All right. Drop in at my office about twelve-thirty. If Mr. Rolsted does accept my invitation, we'll try to find out something about Josiah Crowley's wills." Mr. Drew pushed back his chair. "I must hurry now or I'll be late getting downtown."

After her father had left, Nancy finished her breakfast, then went to the kitchen to help Hannah Gruen, who had already left the table.

"Any errands for me?" Nancy asked.

"Yes, dear. Here's a list," the housekeeper replied. "And good luck with your detective work."

Hannah Gruen gazed at the girl affectionately and several thoughts raced through her mind. In school Nancy had been very popular and had made many friends. But through no fault of her own, she had made two enemies, Ada and Isabel Topham. This worried Hannah. The sisters, intensely jealous of Nancy, had tried to discredit her in positions she had held in school. But loyal friends had always sprung to Nancy's defense. As a result, Ada and Isabel had become more unpleasant than ever to Nancy.

"Thanks for your encouragement," she said to Hannah a little later, giving her a hug.

"Whatever you do, Nancy, beware of those Topham sisters. They'd be only too happy to make things difficult for you."

"I promise to be on my guard."

Before leaving the house, Nancy phoned the Turners. She was glad to hear that Judy had suffered no ill effects from her fall. But she was disappointed that the police had found no clue to the thieves who had stolen the silverware.

"Please let me know if you learn anything," Nancy said, and Edna promised to do so.

Becomingly dressed in a tan cotton suit, Nancy set off in her convertible for the shopping district. She drove down the boulevard, and upon reaching the more congested streets, made her way skillfully through heavy traffic, then pulled into a parking lot.

"I think I'll try Taylor's Department Store first for a dress," she decided.

Taylor's was one of River Heights' finest stores. Nancy purchased several items for Hannah on the main floor, then went directly to the misses' wearing apparel section on the second floor.

Usually Nancy had no trouble finding a salesclerk. But this particular morning seemed to be an especially busy one in the department, and an extra rush of customers had temporarily overwhelmed the sales force.

Nancy sat down in a convenient chair to await her turn. Her thoughts wandered to the Turner sisters and little Judy. Would she be able to help them? She was suddenly brought out of her reverie by loud-voiced complaints.

"We've been standing here nearly ten minutes!" a shrill voice declared. "Send a saleswoman to us immediately!"

Nancy turned to see Ada and Isabel Topham speaking to the floor manager.

"I'm afraid I can't," the man replied regretfully. "There are a number of others ahead of you. All our salespeople are—"

"Perhaps you don't know who we are!" Ada interrupted rudely.

"Indeed I do," the floor manager told her wearily. "I will have a saleswoman here in a few moments. If you will only wait—"

"We're not accustomed to waiting," Isabel Topham told him icily.

"Such service!" Ada chimed in. "Do you realize that my father owns considerable stock in Taylor's? If we report your conduct to him, he could have you discharged."

"I'm sorry," the harassed man apologized. "But it is a rule of the store. You must await your turn."

Ada tossed her head and her eyes flashed angrily. This did nothing to improve her looks. In spite of the expensive clothes she wore, Ada was not attractive. She was very thin and sallow, with an expression of petulance. Now that her face was distorted with anger, she was almost ugly.

Isabel, the pride of the Topham family, was rather pretty, but her face lacked character. She had acquired an artificially elegant manner of speaking which, although irritating, was sometimes amusing. It was her mother's ambition that Isabel marry into a socially prominent family.

"I pity any future husband of hers!" Nancy thought with a chuckle.

Suddenly Ada and Isabel saw Nancy, who nodded a greeting. Isabel coldly returned the nod, but Ada gave no indication that she had even noticed Nancy.

At that moment a saleswoman hurried toward

the Topham sisters. At once they began to shower
abuse upon the young woman for her failure to
wait on them sooner.

"What is it you wish to look at, Miss Topham?"
the clerk said, flushing.

"Evening dresses."

The saleswoman brought out several dresses.
Nancy watched curiously as the Tophams, in an
unpleasant frame of mind, tossed aside beautiful
models with scarcely a second glance. They found
fault with every garment.

"This is a very chic gown," the saleswoman told
them hopefully, as she displayed a particularly
attractive dress of lace and chiffon. "It arrived
only this morning."

Ada picked it up, gave the dress one careless
glance, then tossed it into a chair, as the distracted
clerk went off to bring other frocks.

The fluffy gown slipped to the floor in a
crumpled mass. To Nancy's horror Ada stepped
on it as she turned to examine another dress. In
disgust, Nancy went to pick it up.

"Leave that alone!" Ada cried out, her eyes blaz-
ing. "Nobody asked for your help."

"Are you buying this?" Nancy asked evenly.

"It's none of your business!"

As Nancy continued to hold the dress, Ada in a
rage snatched it from her hands, causing a long
tear in the chiffon skirt.

"Oh!" Isabel cried out. "Now you've done it! We'd better get out of here, Ada!"

"And why?" her haughty sister shrilled. "It was Nancy Drew's fault! She's always making trouble."

"It was *not* my fault," Nancy said.

"Come on, Ada," Isabel urged, "before that clerk gets back."

Reluctantly Ada followed Isabel out of the department. As they rushed toward a waiting elevator, Nancy gazed after them. At this moment the saleswoman reappeared with an armful of lovely frocks. She stared in bewilderment at the torn dress.

"Where did my customers go?" she asked Nancy worriedly.

Nancy pointed toward the elevator, but made no comment. Instead she said, "I'm looking for an evening dress myself. This torn one is very pretty. Do you think it could be mended?"

"Oh, I don't know," the woebegone clerk wailed. "I'll probably be held responsible and I can't afford to pay for the dress."

"I'm sure Taylor's wouldn't ask you to do that," Nancy said kindly. "If there's any trouble, I'll speak to the manager myself. What usually happens is that such a dress is greatly reduced."

"Thank you," the clerk replied. "I'll call Miss Reed, the fitter, and see what can be done."

"First, let me try on the dress," Nancy said, smiling.

They found a vacant fitting room and Nancy took off her suit and blouse. Then she slipped the lovely pale-blue dance creation over her head and the saleswoman zipped it up.

"It's darling on you," she said enthusiastically.

Nancy grinned. "I kind of like myself in it," she said. "Please call the fitter now."

Presently Miss Reed, a gray-haired woman, appeared. Within seconds she had made a change in an overlap of the chiffon skirt. The tear was no longer visible and the style of the dress was actually improved.

"I told our manager what happened," said the saleswoman. "If you want the dress, he will reduce the price fifty percent."

"How wonderful!" Nancy exclaimed. Laughing, she said, "That price will fit into my budget nicely. I'll take the dress. Please send it." She gave her name and address. To herself she added, "Ada Topham did me a favor. But if she ever finds out what happened, she'll certainly be burned up!" Nancy suppressed a giggle.

"It's been a real pleasure waiting on you, Miss Drew," the saleswoman said after Miss Reed left and Nancy was putting on her suit. "But how I dread to see those Topham sisters come in here! They're so unreasonable. And they'll be even worse when they get Josiah Crowley's money."

The woman lowered her voice. "The estate hasn't been settled, but the girls are counting on the fortune already. Last week I heard Ada say to her sister, 'Oh, I guess there's no question about our getting old Crowley's fortune. But I wish Father would stop worrying that somebody is going to show up with a later will which may do us out of it.'"

Nancy was too discreet to engage in gossip with the saleswoman. But she was interested and excited about the information. The fact that Mr. Topham was disturbed indicated to her that he too suspected Josiah Crowley had made a second will!

The conversation reminded Nancy of her date. She glanced at her wrist watch and saw that it was after twelve o'clock.

"I must hurry or I'll be late for an appointment with my dad," she told the saleswoman.

Nancy drove directly to her father's office. Although she was a few minutes ahead of the appointed time, she found that he was ready to leave.

"What luck, Dad?" Nancy asked eagerly. "Did Mr. Rolsted accept your luncheon invitation?"

"Yes. We are to meet him at the Royal Hotel in ten minutes. Do you still think I should quiz him about the Crowley will?"

"Oh, I'm more interested than ever in the case." She told her father about the saleswoman's gossipy remarks.

"Hm," said Mr. Drew. "It's not what you'd call evidence, but the old saying usually holds good, 'Where there's smoke, there's fire.' Come, let's go!"

The Royal Hotel was located less than a block away, and Nancy and her father quickly walked the distance. Mr. Rolsted was waiting in the lobby. Carson Drew introduced his daughter, then the three made their way to the dining room where a table had been reserved for them.

At first the conversation centered about a variety of subjects. As the luncheon progressed the two lawyers talked enthusiastically of their college days together and finally of their profession. Nancy began to fear that the subject of the Crowley estate might never be brought up.

Then, after the dessert course, Mr. Drew skillfully turned the conversation into a new channel and mentioned some strange cases which he had handled.

"By the way," he said, "I haven't heard the details of the Crowley case. How are the Tophams making out? I understand other relatives are trying to break the will."

For a moment Mr. Rolsted remained silent. Was he reluctant to enter into a discussion of the matter? Nancy wondered.

Finally the lawyer said quietly, "The settlement of the estate wasn't given to me, Carson. But I confess I've followed it rather closely because of something that happened a year ago. As the present will stands, I do not believe it can be broken."

"Then the Tophams fall heir to the entire estate," Mr. Drew commented.

"Yes, unless a more recent will is uncovered."

"Another will?" Carson Drew inquired innocently. "Then you believe Crowley made a second one?"

Mr. Rolsted hesitated as though uncertain whether or not he should divulge any further information. Then, with a quick glance about, he lowered his voice and said, "Of course this is strictly confidential—"

CHAPTER IV

Racing the Storm

"CONFIDENTIAL?" Mr. Drew repeated, looking at Mr. Rolsted. "You may rest assured that whatever you tell us will not be repeated to anyone."

"Well, I'll say this much," Mr. Rolsted went on, "about a year ago Josiah Crowley came to me and said he wanted to draw up a new will. He indicated that he intended to spread out his bequests among several people. He expressed a desire to write the will himself, and asked me a number of questions. I took him to my office and told him exactly how to proceed. When he left, he promised to have me look over the document after he had drawn it up."

"Then you actually saw the will?" Mr. Drew asked in surprise.

"No. Strange to say, Crowley never came back. I don't know whether he ever wrote the will or not."

"And if he did, there would be a chance that it would not be legal?" Nancy spoke up.

"Yes. He might have typed it and signed the paper without a witness. In this state at least two witnesses are required and three are advisable."

"What would happen," Nancy asked, "if a person were ill or dying and had no witness, and wanted to make a will?"

Mr. Rolsted smiled. "That sometimes happens. If the person writes the will himself by hand and signs it, so there's no doubt the same person did both, the surrogate's office will accept it for probate."

"Then if Mr. Crowley wrote out and signed a new will, it would be legal," Nancy commented.

"That's right. But there's another thing to remember. It's pretty risky for someone who is not a lawyer to draw up a will that cannot be broken."

Mr. Drew nodded. "If Josiah Crowley left any loophole in a will he wrote personally, the Tophams would drag the matter into court."

"Yes. It's a foregone conclusion that the Tophams will fight to keep the fortune whether they have a right to it or not. I believe some other relatives have filed a claim, but up to the moment they have no proof that a later will exists."

Although Nancy gave no indication of her feelings, the possibility that Mr. Crowley had made a new will thrilled her. As soon as Mr. Drew paid the luncheon check, the three arose and left the dining room.   Mr. Rolsted took leave of Nancy and her father in the lobby.

"Well, Nancy, did you find out what you wanted to know?" Mr. Drew asked after the lawyer had left.

"Oh, Dad, it's just as I suspected.   I'm sure Mr. Crowley did make a later will!   He hid it some place!   If only I could find out where!"

"It would be like looking for a needle in a haystack," Mr. Drew commented.

"I must figure out a way!" Nancy said with determination.   "I want to help little Judy."

She awoke the next morning thinking about the mystery.   But where should she start hunting for possible clues to a second will?   She continued pondering about it while she showered and dressed.

As she entered the dining room, she was greeted with a cheery "Good morning" from her father and Hannah Gruen.   During breakfast Mr. Drew said, "Nancy, would you do a little errand for me this morning?"

"Why, of course, Dad."

"I have a number of legal documents which must be delivered to Judge Hart at Masonville some time before noon.   I'd take them myself, but I have several important appointments.   I'd appreciate it if you would drive over there with them."

"I'll be glad to go," Nancy promised willingly.

"Besides, it's such a wonderful day. I'll enjoy the trip. Where are the papers?"

"At the office. You can drive me down and I'll get them for you."

Nancy, wearing a yellow sunback dress and jacket, hurried away to get her gloves and handbag. Before Mr. Drew had collected his own belongings, she had brought her car from the garage and was waiting for him at the front door.

"I put the top down so I can enjoy the sun," she explained as her father climbed in.

"Good idea. I haven't heard you mention the Crowley case yet today," Mr. Drew teased as they rode along. "Have you forgotten about it?"

Nancy's face clouded. "No, I haven't forgotten, but I must admit I *am* stumped as to where to search for clues."

"Maybe I can help you. I've learned that the two girls on River Road who expected to be remembered in the will are named Hoover. You might look them up on your return trip."

"That's great. I'll watch the mailboxes for their name."

When they reached the building where Mr. Drew had his office, Nancy parked the car and waited while her father went upstairs to get the legal documents to be delivered to Judge Hart. Returning a few minutes later, he placed a fat Manila envelope in his daughter's hand.

"Give this to the judge. You know where to find him?"

"Yes, Dad. In the old Merchants Trust Company Building."

"That's right."

Selecting a recently constructed highway, Nancy rode along, glancing occasionally at the neatly planted fields on either side. Beyond were rolling hills.

"Pretty," she commented to herself. "Oh, why can't all people be nice like this scenery and not make trouble?"

It was nearly eleven o'clock when she finally drove into Masonville. Nancy went at once to Judge Hart's office but was informed he had gone to the courthouse. Recalling that her father had mentioned the necessity of the papers being delivered before noon, she set off in search of the judge.

Nancy had considerable trouble trying to see him, and it was twelve o'clock when at last she delivered the Manila envelope into his hands.

"Thank you very much," he said. "I'll need these directly after lunch."

Nancy smiled. "Then I'm glad I found you."

When Judge Hart learned that Nancy was the daughter of Carson Drew, he at once insisted that she have luncheon with him and his wife at their home before returning to River Heights.

She accepted the invitation and spent a very

pleasant hour with the Harts. During the meal the judge laughingly asked if Nancy was still playing aide to her father.

"Oh, yes," she said, and at once told him about the Drews' interest in the Crowley case.

"Did you know Josiah Crowley or ever hear of him?" she asked.

Both the Harts nodded. "A maid who used to be with them, came to work for us after Mrs. Crowley's death," the judge explained. "Jane herself passed away a short time ago."

"We never met Josiah," Mrs. Hart added, "but Jane pointed him out to my husband and me one time down on Main Street."

"Did he have relatives or friends in town?" Nancy inquired.

"I think not," the judge replied.

Nancy wondered what old Josiah had been doing in Masonville if he had no relatives or friends there. The town was not known as a spot for sight-seeing. Her interest was further quickened when Mrs. Hart remarked that she had seen Mr. Crowley in town at another time also.

"How long ago was that?" the girl asked.

Mrs. Hart thought a minute, then replied, "Oh, less than a year, I'd say."

When luncheon was over, the judge said he must leave. Nancy told the Harts she too should go. She thanked them for their hospitality, then said good-by. Soon she was driving homeward.

"Why had Mr. Crowley gone to Masonville?" she asked herself. "Could it have had anything to do with a later will?"

Nancy had chosen a route which would take her to River Road. Half an hour later she turned into the beautiful country road which wound in and out along the Muskoka River, and began to look at the names on the mailboxes. "Hoover," she reminded herself.

About halfway to River Heights, while enjoying the pastoral scenes of cows standing knee-high in shallow sections of the stream, and sheep grazing on flower-dotted hillsides, Nancy suddenly realized the sun had been blotted out.

"A thunderstorm's on the way," she told herself, glancing at black clouds scudding across the sky. "Guess I'd better put the top of the car up."

She pressed the button on the dashboard to raise the top, but nothing happened. Puzzled, Nancy tried again. Still there was no response. By this time large drops of rain had started to fall.

"I'll get soaked," Nancy thought, as she looked around.

There was no shelter in sight. But ahead, past a steep rise, was a sharp bend in the road. Hopeful that there would be a house or barn beyond, Nancy started the car again.

Vivid forked lightning streaked across the sky. It was followed by an earth-shaking clap of thunder. The rain came down harder,

"Oh, why didn't I bring a raincoat?" Nancy wailed.

When Nancy swung around the bend, she was delighted to see a barn with lightning rods about a quarter mile ahead. Farther on stood a small white house.

"I wonder if that's the Hoover place," Nancy mused.

By now the storm was letting loose in all its fury. The sky was as dark as night and Nancy had to switch on her headlights to see the road. She was already thoroughly drenched and her thought of shelter at this point was one of safety rather than of keeping dry.

Nancy turned on the windshield wipers, but the rain was so blinding in its intensity, it was impossible to see more than a few feet ahead. Almost in an instant the road had dissolved into a sea of mud.

Nancy had been caught in a number of storms, but never one as violent as this. She feared a bad skid might land her in a ditch before she could reach the shelter of the barn.

"How much farther is it?" she worried. "It didn't seem this far away."

The next instant, to Nancy's right, a ball of fire rocketed down from the sky.

"Oh! That was close!" she thought fearfully. Her skin tingled from the electrical vibrations in the air.

A moment later a surge of relief swept over Nancy. "At last!" she breathed.

At the side of the road the barn loomed up. Its large double doors were wide open. Without hesitation, Nancy headed straight for the building and drove in.

The next moment she heard a piercing scream!

CHAPTER V

A Surprising Story

NANCY froze behind the wheel. Had she inadvertently hit someone? Her heart pounding in fright, she opened the car door to step out.

At the same instant a shadowy figure arose from a pile of hay near her. "I guess I must have scared you silly when I screamed," said a girl of Nancy's age, stepping forward.

"You— You're all right?" Nancy gasped.

"Yes. And I'm sorry I yelled. I came out here to check on our supply of feed for the chickens. I didn't think it was going to be a bad storm, so I didn't bother to go back to the house."

"It's pretty bad," said Nancy.

"Well, the storm terrified me," the girl continued. "I didn't hear your car coming, and when it rushed in here, I panicked."

Nancy began to breathe normally again, then

told the stranger her name and the fact that the mechanism for raising the top of the convertible was not working.

"That's a shame," said the girl. "And you must get your clothes dried. The storm is letting up. Let's dash over to the house. Grace will help you too. She's my sister. My name's Allison Hoover."

Hoover! Nancy was tempted to tell Allison that she had been planning to call, but she decided not to mention it at the moment. It might be better to do her sleuthing more subtly.

Nancy smiled at Allison. "Thanks a million. But first I'd like to wipe out the car. Are there any rags around the barn?"

Allison produced several and together the two girls mopped the water from the cushions and floor. By this time the rain had stopped. As Nancy and Allison sloshed through a series of puddles to the farmhouse, Nancy had a better chance to study her companion. She was tall, with reddish-blond hair and very fair skin. Her voice was musical and she had an attractive, lilting laugh.

The girls reached the run-down farmhouse and stamped the mud from their shoes on the back porch. Then Allison flung open the door, and they entered a cheerful kitchen.

As the door shut behind them, another girl who was just closing the oven of an old-fashioned range turned toward them in surprise.

"Grace, I've brought a visitor," Allison said

quickly. "Nancy, I want you to meet my sister. She's the mainstay of our family of two."

Grace Hoover cordially acknowledged the introduction and greeted Nancy with a warm smile. Nancy judged her to be at least four years older than Allison. Her face was rather serious, and it was evident from her manner that responsibility had fallen on her shoulders at an early age.

Nancy was attracted to both girls and responded to their friendly welcome. She put on a robe which Allison brought her and Grace hung her wet clothes near the range. Presently Grace pulled an ironing board from a closet with the intention of pressing Nancy's garments. But Nancy would not hear of this and began to iron them herself.

"This is fun," she said to the sisters. "I don't know what I would have done without you girls."

"It's great for us," Allison spoke up. "We don't have much company. To tell you the truth, we can't afford it."

Grace stepped to the stove, removed a golden-brown cake from the oven, and set it on the table to cool.

"But today we're not talking about money. It's Allison's birthday and this is a birthday cake. Nancy, if you're not in too much of a hurry, I wish you'd join us in a little celebration."

"Why, I'd love to," Nancy said.

"Grace's cakes are yummy," Allison declared.

"I'm not much of a cook myself. My department is taking care of the barn and the chickens."

Soon Nancy finished pressing her clothes and put them back on. Meanwhile, the cake had cooled and Grace started to spread the chocolate frosting.

"Suppose you two go into the living room and wait," she suggested. "I'll bring in the cake and tea."

Nancy followed Allison to the adjoining room. Although it was comfortable, the room did not contain much furniture. The floor had been painted and was scantily covered with handmade rag rugs. With the exception of an old-fashioned sofa, an inexpensive table, a few straight-backed chairs and an old oil stove which furnished heat in cold weather, there was little else in the room. However, dainty white curtains covered the windows, and Nancy realized that although the Hoovers were poor, they had tried hard to make their home attractive.

"Do you two girls live here alone all the time?" Nancy inquired.

Allison nodded. "Grace and I have been living here since Father died. That was two years ago. Mother passed away just before that," the girl added with a slight catch in her voice. "Their illnesses took every penny we had."

"I'm terribly sorry," Nancy remarked sympathetically. "It must be dreadfully hard for two girls to run the farm by themselves."

"Our farm isn't as large as it once was," Allison said quietly. "We have only a few acres left. I know you are too polite to ask how we manage, Nancy. Grace helps a dressmaker at Masonville whenever she can get work. She makes all her own clothes and mine too. And I raise chickens."

From just beyond the doorway suddenly came the strains of "Happy Birthday to you! Happy Birth—"

By this time Nancy had joined in. She and Grace finished "—day to you. Happy Birthday, dear Allison. Happy Birthday to you!"

Grace set the cake with eighteen lighted candles on the table. She and Nancy sang the second verse with the words "May you have many more!"

Tears stood in Allison's eyes. When the song ended, she grasped her sister in a tremendous hug. Then she gave Nancy one.

"This—this is the nicest birthday I've had in years," she quavered.

"And it's one of the most enjoyable I've ever attended," Nancy said sincerely.

Suddenly Allison began to sing a tuneful old English ballad about the birthday of a village lass. Nancy listened entranced to Allison's clear, bell-like tones. When she finished, Nancy applauded, then said:

"That was perfectly lovely. You have a beautiful voice, Allison!"

The singer laughed gaily. "Thank you, Nancy. I've always wanted to take lessons, but as you know, voice training is pretty expensive."

At that moment Grace brought in a tray of fragrant tea. As she poured three cups, Allison blew out the candles and served the cake.

"I've never tasted anything more delicious in all my life," Nancy said enthusiastically.

The three girls chatted like old friends. Finally the sun broke through the clouds. As Nancy rose to leave, she noticed an unusual picture on the wall opposite her and commented on its beauty.

"Uncle Josiah Crowley gave it to us," Allison told her. "If he were only alive now, things would be different."

At the mention of the name, Nancy sat down again. Was she going to pick up a clue to the possibility that Mr. Crowley had made a later will?

"He wasn't really our uncle," Grace explained. "But we loved him as much as though he were a relative." Her voice broke and for a moment she could not go on. Then, gaining control of herself, she continued, "He lived on the farm next to us— that was when Mother and Father were alive. All of Allison's and my misfortunes seemed to come at once."

"He was the dearest man you ever saw," Allison

added. "Some people thought him queer, but you never minded his peculiar ways after you knew him. Uncle Josiah was very good to us. He always told me that he'd back me in a singing career."

"Yes," Grace added. "Uncle Josiah used to say Allison sang as sweetly as a bird and he wanted to pay for lessons with a famous teacher. But after he went to live with the Tophams, he never said any more about it."

"He never liked it with the Tophams, though," Allison declared. "They weren't kind to him, and he used to slip away to visit us."

"Uncle Josiah often said that we seemed like his own children," Grace spoke up. "He brought us many nice gifts, but we loved him for himself and not his money. I remember, though, the very last day we saw him alive, he told us 'I have planned a big surprise to make you girls happy. But I can't tell you now what it is. You'll see it in my will.' Those were his very words."

"And then the Tophams got everything," Allison said. "He must have changed his mind for some reason."

"It's hard to believe he would forget his promise to us," Grace said sadly.

"Oh, wouldn't it be wonderful if a later will could be found!" Allison exclaimed.

"Yes," Nancy replied slowly. "I've heard that

Mr. Crowley told other people he was leaving money to them. The Turner sisters, for instance. Do you know them?"

"Slightly," Grace answered.

"My dad," Nancy went on, "is a lawyer and he and I are very much interested in this case. He even mentioned you girls, and to tell the truth I was on my way here to talk to you."

Allison impulsively grasped Nancy's arm. "You say your father is a lawyer? Grace and I are positive Uncle Josiah made a later will. Oh, if we could only engage your father to help us prove this!" Then a sad look came over her face. "But I'm forgetting—we wouldn't have any money to pay him if we should lose the case."

"Don't let that worry you," said Nancy kindly. "This is your birthday and you must be happy, Allison. My special wish for you is that before you're one year older, you'll inherit some of the Crowley money, so that you can take those singing lessons!"

CHAPTER VI

An Exciting Appointment

THE HOOVER girls walked out to the barn with Nancy. "Do come to see us again," Grace called, as the young detective climbed into her car.

"Yes, please do," Allison added.

Nancy promised that she would. "As soon as I have some news," she said.

Although the weather had cleared, the River Road remained muddy and slippery. Nancy found it necessary to drive with extreme care for the next two miles until she reached the main highway.

"No wonder this River Road isn't used much," she thought. "And how do Grace and Allison get to town?" Nancy wondered. She had not seen a car at the Hoover home and knew that no bus passed their door.

"I certainly wish," she thought, "that I or somebody else could locate a later will of Josiah Crowley's by which the Hoovers and the Turners would receive some much-needed money. I must tell Dad about this latest development."

She decided to see if her father was in his office and drove directly there. Nancy parked the car in a nearby lot. She surveyed the convertible ruefully as she climbed out.

"Poor thing! It certainly needs a bath!"

Nancy found Mr. Drew in. As she entered his private office, he arose from the desk chair to kiss her. "I'm glad you're here—and safe," the lawyer said. "I was worried about you when that violent storm came up. When Hannah phoned me that you weren't back, I began to regret I'd sent you on the errand."

His daughter grinned. "I'm back, all in one piece. I delivered the papers to Judge Hart and learned that he and his wife saw Mr. Crowley in Masonville a couple of times. Also, I talked to the Hoover girls."

She described her meeting with Allison and Grace Hoover and ended by asking her father if he could help them.

"From what you say, it does look as though Josiah Crowley might have made another will which included them as beneficiaries," Mr. Drew commented thoughtfully. "I'll be glad to do anything I can to help the Hoover girls."

He asked whether the sisters had given Nancy any specific information about Mr. Crowley's habits or other helpful clues. When Nancy shook her head, Mr. Drew suggested that she invite the girls to his office for a little conference. "Perhaps if I ask them some questions, it will recall helpful incidents." The lawyer studied his desk calendar for a moment, then looked up at his daughter. "How about tomorrow afternoon at two-forty-five? I can give them about half an hour."

For answer, Nancy gave her father a hug and then asked if she might use his telephone to call the Hoovers at once.

Grace and Allison eagerly accepted the Drews' invitation, and Nancy said she would drive out to bring them to the conference and take them home afterward.

"You're a doll!" cried Allison, who had answered the telephone. "Nancy, I just know you're going to solve this mystery!"

Suddenly an idea came to Nancy. She asked Allison how long the girls would be able to stay in River Heights.

"Oh, as long as you need us," Allison replied.

"Good. Then I'd like you both to stay and have supper with us," Nancy said.

"Sorry I can't join you," Mr. Drew told his daughter as she hung up. "I have a dinner engagement and conference in the evening."

Just then, the mayor of River Heights was shown into the lawyer's office, and Nancy arose to leave. She spoke to the mayor for a moment, then said, "See you later, Dad."

Before Nancy returned home, she stopped at an old-fashioned house on a side street. It was the home of Signor Mascagni, a famous voice teacher who had retired to the small city the year before, but took a few outstanding pupils. Nancy introduced herself to the white bushy-haired, florid-faced man, then said:

"Signor Mascagni, would you be willing to listen to the voice of a friend of mine and give your honest opinion as to whether or not she might become a great singer? If she might, and she can obtain the money for lessons, would you be able to take her as a pupil?"

Signor Mascagni studied Nancy for several minutes before replying. Finally he said, "You do not look like the kind of girl who would come here on a foolish errand. Ordinarily I do not accept beginners. But in this case I would be willing to hear your friend sing." He laughed. "Mind you, I will give you nothing but the truth, and if your friend does not measure up, I hope her feelings will not be hurt too deeply."

Nancy laughed too. "I like honesty," she said. "As a matter of fact, this girl knows nothing about what I am asking you. Coming here will be a complete surprise to her. I'm probably no judge of voices, but I think she's a natural. However, we will both appreciate having your opinion, and will certainly abide by it."

She arranged for a meeting the following after-

noon at four o'clock and left Signor Mascagni's
house in an excited mood. "Maybe I'm going way
out on a limb," Nancy mused, "but this is another
one of those hunches of mine that Dad talks about,
and I must carry through."

When she picked up the Hoovers the following
day, Nancy did not mention the appointment with
the voice teacher. The three girls went directly
to Mr. Drew's office and at once he began to quiz
Grace and Allison about Mr. Crowley.

"I understand that he was a rather eccentric
man," the lawyer began. "Suppose you tell me
everything you can remember about what Josiah
Crowley did and what he said which would help
us figure out where he might have secreted a later
will."

"Uncle Josiah was rather absent-minded," Grace
spoke up. "I often saw him hunting for his spec-
tacles, which he had pushed up on his head."

"Did he ever hide things?" Mr. Drew asked.

"Oh, yes." Allison laughed. "Uncle Josiah
was always putting articles away in what he called
a safe place. But the places were so safe he never
could find the things again!"

"Then," Nancy spoke up excitedly, "Mr. Crowley could have hidden a will and then forgotten
where?"

"I suppose so," Grace replied. "While living
with the Tophams, I'm sure that's just what he
would have done. One day when he was calling at

our house he talked about the Tophams and the way they were trying to get all his money. 'I guess they think—just because I stay on—that they're going to get everything. But they'll be fooled when they find I've made another will,' he said with that odd little chuckle of his. 'This time I'm not going to trust it to any lawyer. I'll put it away in a place that I know will be safe.' "

Allison asked Mr. Drew, "Do you think Uncle Josiah hid another will somewhere in the Tophams' house?"

The lawyer looked down at his desk for several seconds before replying. "If he did, we would have a great fight on our hands, I'm afraid, trying to persuade the Tophams to let us make a search."

Another thought had come to Nancy and she shuddered at the idea. Perhaps the Tophams had been alerted by all the talk of a later will, had searched for it, discovered one, and by now destroyed it!

She flashed her father a questioning look and got the impression that he had the same thought. But there was no point in discouraging the Hoover girls by telling them this.

Mr. Drew continued to question the sisters until three-thirty, then said he had another appointment. He would do all he could to help the girls and would not charge them for his services.

"Unless they bring results," he added with a smile.

"You're very kind, just like your daughter," said Grace as she arose and shook hands with the lawyer. "You have no idea how much Allison and I appreciate what you're doing for us."

When the three girls reached Nancy's car, she told the sisters she wanted them to meet someone special in town, and drove directly to Signor Mascagni's home. As they went up to the front porch they could hear the sounds of a soprano voice singing an aria from *Tosca*.

"How beautiful!" Allison exclaimed softly.

The girls were admitted by a maid and asked to wait in a small room while Signor Mascagni's pupil finished her lesson. Puzzled, Allison waited for Nancy to explain.

"I have a surprise for you," Nancy said with a grin. "Signor Mascagni has promised to listen to your voice. If you pass the test, he'll consider taking you as a pupil—that is, after we find the money for voice lessons."

Allison was too dumfounded to speak, but Grace cried out, "Oh, Nancy, what are you going to do next? We've known you only twenty-four hours and you've already boosted our morale sky-high."

At this moment the door to the studio opened. The young soprano came out, followed by Signor Mascagni. He said good-by to his pupil, then invited the three callers into the studio. Nancy quickly introduced the Hoover sisters.

"And you are the singer," the man said almost

at once, addressing Allison. "I can tell from your speaking voice."

Apparently the teacher sensed that Allison had been taken by surprise and was a little nervous. Accordingly he began to talk on other subjects than music. He showed the girls several paintings in the room and pieces of statuary which had come from Italy.

"I prize them highly," he said.

"They are exquisite," Allison remarked.

Signor Mascagni walked to a rear window and pointed out a lovely garden in back of the house. Then, evidently satisfied that Allison was at ease, he led the way to the grand piano and sat down.

"Now what would you like to sing?" he asked Allison with a smile. "Please stand right here facing me."

"Something very simple," she replied. " 'America the Beautiful'?"

The teacher nodded, asked her what key she would like it played in, then began to accompany her. Allison sang as though inspired. Her voice sounded even more beautiful than it had at the farmhouse, Nancy thought. When Allison finished the song, Signor Mascagni made no comment. Instead he asked her to try a scale, then to sing single tones, jumping from octave to octave.

"You have a very fine range, Miss Hoover," was his only comment.

For half an hour he had Allison try short songs

in various keys and at one point joined with her in a duet. At last he turned around on the piano bench and faced Nancy and Grace.

"I believe," he said slowly, "I believe that some day we shall know Allison Hoover as an operatic star!"

Before the girls could say anything, he jumped up and turned to shake Allison's hand fervently. By this time the full import of his words had dawned on the young singer. Tears began to roll down her cheeks.

"*Bravissimo! Bravissimo!*" he exclaimed. "You sing, you cry, you smile! *Magnifico!* You will also be a dramatic actress *splendida.*"

Nancy and Grace were nearly on the verge of tears also, they were so overwhelmed by the happy news. Then suddenly the three girls became serious, remembering that there was still the problem of money for lessons from this great man. They knew his fee per hour must be very high.

Allison suddenly began to talk and poured out her whole story to the white-haired teacher. "But I know," she declared with a brave smile, "that somehow I'm going to get the money for the lessons and I wouldn't want to take them from anybody but you, Signor Mascagni. I'll come back to you just as soon as I can. Thank you very, very much. Please, girls, I'd like to leave now."

As Allison rushed toward the front door, Signor Mascagni detained Nancy and Grace. "This Allison, she is wonderful!" he exclaimed. "I want to give her lessons to see that her training is correct." He threw up his hands and shook his head. "But I cannot afford to give the lessons free. Perhaps I could cut my price—"

"We'll find the money somehow, signor!" Nancy promised. Then she and Grace thanked the teacher and followed Allison outside.

At the Drew home that evening there were mixed emotions on everyone's part. Hannah Gruen had taken a great fancy to the Hoover sisters and the news of Allison's talent had thrilled her, as well as the girls. Conversation at supper was gay and animated. Nancy and Mrs. Gruen drove the sisters to their farm and on parting Nancy again promised to do all she could to help find a will from which the girls might possibly benefit.

But figuring out how to do this became a problem that seemed insurmountable to Nancy. At breakfast the following day, Mr. Drew suggested, "Nancy, perhaps if you'd give your mind a little rest from the Crowley matter, an inspiration about the case might come to you."

His daughter smiled. "Good idea, Dad. I think I'll take a walk in the fresh air and clear the cobwebs from my brain."

As soon as she finished eating, Nancy set out at a brisk pace. She headed for River Heights' attractive park to view the display of roses which was

Signor Muscugni shook Allison's hand fervently

always very beautiful. She had gone only a short distance along one of the paths when she caught sight of Isabel and Ada Topham seated on a bench not far ahead.

"They're the last people in the world I want to see right now," Nancy thought. "They'll probably say something mean to me and I'll lose my temper. When I think how Grace and Allison and the Turners could use just one-tenth of the Crowley money which the Tophams are going to inherit, I could just burst!"

Nancy had paused, wondering whether she should turn back. "No," she told herself, "I'll go on to see the roses. I'll take that path back of the Tophams and they won't notice me."

Nancy made her way along quietly, with no intention of eavesdropping on the two girls. But suddenly two words of their conversation came to her ears, bringing Nancy to an involuntary halt.

She had distinctly heard Isabel say—"the will."

In a flash Nancy's detective instincts were aroused and her heart pounded excitedly. " It must be Josiah Crowley's will they're talking about," she reasoned.

CHAPTER VII

The Angry Dog

WITH the instinct of a detective who dared not miss a clue, Nancy deliberately moved closer to the bench on which the Topham girls were seated.

"If there *should* be another will, I'm afraid we'd be out of luck." The words, in Ada's nasal voice, came clearly to Nancy.

Isabel's reply was in so low a tone that the young sleuth could just manage to catch the words, "Well, I, for one, don't believe Josiah Crowley ever made a later will." She gave a low laugh. "Mother watched him like a hawk."

"Or thought she did," Isabel retorted. "The old man got out of her clutches several times, don't forget."

"Yes, and what's worse, I'm sure Nancy Drew thinks he made a later will. That's why she's taking such an interest in those Hoover girls. I actually saw them go into Mr. Drew's office yesterday and it wasn't to deliver eggs!   If Nancy gets her father interested, he might dig up another will. Oh, how I hate that interfering girl!"

At this Nancy could barely refrain from laughing.   So the Tophams *were* concerned about the existence of a second will.   With bated breath she listened further.

"You're such a worry wart, Ada.   You can trust Dad and Mother to take care of things, no matter what happens," Isabel commented dryly.   "They won't let that pile of money get away from us.   It's ours by right, anyhow."

"You've got something there," Ada conceded. "We should have old Josiah's money after supporting and putting up with him for three years. That was pretty clever of Mother, never accepting any board money from Josiah Crowley!"

The conversation ended as Isabel and Ada arose from the bench and walked away.   Nancy waited until they were out of sight, then emerged from her hiding place.   Seating herself on the bench vacated by the Topham sisters, Nancy mulled over the remarks she had just overheard.

"There's no doubt in my mind now that if there is a later will, the Tophams haven't destroyed it. How thrilling!   But where can it be?"

Nancy realized that to find it was a real challenge.   "And I'd better hurry up before the Tophams stumble on it!"

For another ten minutes Nancy sat lost in

thought, sifting all the facts she had gleaned so far.

"There must be some clue I've overlooked," she told herself. Suddenly, with a cry of delight, she sprang to her feet. "Why didn't I think of that before! The Hoover girls and the Turners aren't the only ones who should have figured in this will. There are other relatives of Mr. Crowley who have filed a claim. I wonder who they are. If I could only talk with them, I might pick up a clue!"

Immediately Nancy set off for her father's office. He was engaged in an important conference when she arrived, and she had to wait ten minutes before being admitted to the inner office.

"Now what?" Mr. Drew asked, smiling, as she burst in upon him. "Have you solved the mystery or is your purse in need of a little change?"

Nancy's cheeks were flushed and her eyes danced with excitement. "Don't tease me," she protested. "I need some information!"

"At your service, Nancy."

The young sleuth poured out the story of the Topham sisters' conversation in the park, and told him of her own conclusions. Mr. Drew listened with interest until she had finished.

"Excellent deducting," he praised his daughter. "I'm afraid, though, I can't help you obtain the relatives' names. I don't know any of them."

Nancy looked disappointed. "Oh dear!" she sighed. "And I'm so anxious to find out right away. If I delay even a single day the Tophams may locate that other will—and destroy it."

The next instant her face brightened. "I know! I'll drive out and see the Turner sisters. They might be able to tell me who the other relatives are." Nancy arose and headed for the door.

"Just a minute," said the lawyer. "I wonder if you realize just what you are getting into, Nancy?"

"What do you mean?"

"Only this. Detective work isn't always the safest occupation in which to engage. I happen to know that Richard Topham is an unpleasant man when crossed. If you do find out anything which may frustrate him, the entire Topham family could make things extremely difficult for you."

"I'm not afraid of them, Dad."

"Good!" Mr. Drew exclaimed. "I was hoping you would say that. I'm glad you have the courage of your convictions, but I didn't want you to march off into battle without a knowledge of what you might be up against."

"Battle?"

"Yes. The Tophams won't give up the fortune without a bitter struggle. However, if they attempt to make serious trouble, I promise to deal with them myself."

"And if I do find the will?"

"I'll take the matter into court."

"Oh, thank you! There's no one like you in all the world."

After leaving her father's office, Nancy went directly home to get her car. When she told Hannah Gruen her plans, the housekeeper warned, "Don't become too deeply involved in this matter, dear. In your zeal to help other people, you may forget to be on your guard."

"I promise to be as careful as a pussycat walking up a slippery roof," Nancy assured the housekeeper with a grin, and left the house.

Quickly backing her car from the garage, she set off in the direction of the Turner home. The miles seemed to melt away as Nancy's thoughts raced from one idea to another. Before the young sleuth knew it she had reached the house.

"Hi, Judy!" she called to the little girl, who was playing in the yard with a midget badminton set.

The child looked very cunning in a pink play suit. The hand-embroidered Teddy bears on it were surely the work of her loving aunts.

"Hi, Nancy! I'm glad you came. Now I'll have somebody to play with," Judy said, running up to the visitor.

Obligingly Nancy took a racket and batted the feathered shuttlecock toward the child. "Hit the birdie," she called.

Judy missed but picked up the shuttlecock and whammed it nicely across the net. Nancy hit it back and this time the little girl caught the birdie on her racket and sent it over.

The game went on for several minutes, with

Judy crying out in delight. "You're the bestest batter I ever played with, Nancy," she declared.

After ten minutes of play, Nancy said, "Let's go into the house now, Judy. I want to talk to your aunties."

Judy skipped ahead and announced her new playmate's arrival.

"Hello, Nancy," the women said as she entered the living room.

"We were watching the game from the window," said Mary Turner. "This is a real thrill for Judy. Edna and I are very poor at hitting the birdie."

"It was lots of fun," Nancy replied. "I'm glad to see you all again."

She now asked whether the police had located the thieves who had taken the silver heirlooms from the house.

"Not yet," Mary answered. "And what's worse, we found that several other pieces had been taken too."

"What a shame!" Nancy exclaimed. "But I'm sure the stolen articles will be found." Then she added, "I came here on a particular mission."

"Yes?"

"Your story about Mr. Josiah Crowley intrigued me. Then, the other day, I met two girls, Grace and Allison Hoover, who told me of a similar promise from him regarding his will."

"How amazing!" Edna Turner exclaimed. "I

heard Josiah mention the Hoovers and Allison's beautiful voice."

"Dad and I have become very much interested in the case and are inclined to agree with you and the Hoovers that Mr. Crowley may have written another will shortly before his death and hidden it some place."

"Oh, wouldn't it be wonderful if such a will could be found!" Mary exclaimed. "It might mean all the difference in the world to Judy's future."

"What I want to do," Nancy went on, "is talk to as many of Mr. Crowley's relatives as I can find. Some place I may pick up a clue to where a more recent will is hidden. Tell me, do any of his other relatives live around here?"

"Yes. Three that I can think of," Edna answered.

She went on to say that two cousins, who had never married, lived on a farm just outside Titusville. "Their names are Fred and William Mathews."

Suddenly the Turner sisters blushed a deep pink. They glanced at each other, then back at Nancy. Finally Edna said:

"Many years ago Fred proposed to Mary, and William to me, and we came near accepting. But just at that time we had the great tragedy in the family and took Judy's mother to rear, so we decided not to marry."

An embarrassing pause was broken by Judy. "Some day my aunties are going to give me one of my mother's dollies, Nancy. Isn't that nice?"

"It certainly is," Nancy agreed. "And you must be sure to show it to me." Then she asked the sisters, "What relation are the Mathews to Mr. Crowley?"

"First cousins on his mother's side."

"Do you think they would mind my asking them some questions, even though I'm a stranger?"

"Not at all," Mary replied. "They're very fine gentlemen."

"And tell them Mary and I sent you," Edna added.

"How far is Titusville from here?" Nancy inquired.

"Oh, not more than five miles on Route 10A. You could drive there in a few minutes. It's on the way to Masonville. Nancy, won't you stay and have lunch with us?"

Eager to continue her work, the young sleuth was about to refuse, but Judy put in an invitation also. "Please, oh please, Nancy. And while my aunties are fixing it, you and I can play badminton."

"All right," Nancy agreed. "And thank you very much."

It was nearly two o'clock when she finally was ready to depart.

"Oh, Mary," said Edna suddenly, "we forgot to

tell Nancy about Josiah's wife's cousin, Mrs. Abby Rowen. She'd be apt to know more about the will than anyone else."

"That's right! You really should call on her, Nancy. She took care of Josiah one time when he was sick, and he thought the world of her. He often declared he intended to leave her something. She's a widow and has very little."

"Even a few thousand dollars would mean a lot to her," Edna added. "Abby must be over eighty years of age, and growing forgetful. She has no children and there's no one to look after her."

"Where shall I find Mrs. Rowen?" Nancy asked, hoping it was not far away.

"Abby lives on the West Lake Road," Edna responded. "It's a good many miles from here."

"Then I shan't have time to go there today," the young sleuth said. "But I'll surely see her as soon as I can. And now I must be going."

Nancy thanked the Turner sisters and said good-by. But before she could leave, Judy insisted upon showing how she could jump rope and do all kinds of dancing steps with a hoop on the lawn.

"Judy entertains us all the time," Mary remarked. "We believe she's very talented."

Nancy thought so too. As she drove off, she again hoped that money would become available for a very special education for Judy.

After Nancy had gone five miles along the designated route, she began to watch the mailboxes.

Soon she noticed one which bore the name *Mathews*. The farmhouse stood back a distance from the road and had a wide sweep of lawn in front of it. Near the house a man was riding a small tractor, mowing the grass.

Nancy drove down the narrow lane which led into the grounds, and stopped opposite the spot where the man was working. The man's back was toward her, and he apparently had not heard the car above the noise of the tractor, so she waited.

Looking toward the house, Nancy suddenly saw a sight that appalled her. Wedged between two stones of a broken wall was a police dog puppy whining pitifully. Nancy dashed forward and released the little animal. As it continued to whimper, she cuddled the pup in her arms and began to examine its paws.

"Why, you poor thing!" Nancy said, seeing a tear in the flesh of one hind leg. "This must be taken care of right away."

She decided to carry the puppy over to the man on the mower. As Nancy walked across the lane, she suddenly heard an angry growl near her. Looking back, she saw a huge police dog, evidently the pup's mother, bounding toward her.

"It's all right," Nancy called soothingly to the dog. "I'm not going to take your baby away."

She took two more strides, but got no farther. With a fierce snarl the dog leaped on Nancy, knocking her flat!

CHAPTER VIII

A Forgotten Secret

NANCY screamed for help, hoping to attract the farmer's attention. She expected momentarily to be bitten by the angry dog, but to her great relief the animal did not harm her.

The young sleuth's sudden fall had caused the puppy to fly from her arms. With a leap its mother was at the pup's side. She grabbed her baby by the back of its neck and trotted off toward the barn.

"O-o, that was a narrow escape." Nancy took a deep breath as she got to her feet, brushed herself off, and ruefully surveyed a tear in her sweater.

By this time the man on the tractor, having changed direction, saw the fracas and came running. He apologized for the dog's actions, but Nancy said quickly:

"It was my fault. I should have set the pup

down. Its mother probably thought I was trying to dognap her baby!"

"Possibly."

Nancy explained why she had picked up the little animal and the farmer said he would look at the cut later.

"I'm glad you weren't hurt," he added. "Thanks for being such a good scout about it. Did you come to see me or my brother?" he asked. "I'm Fred Mathews."

Nancy gave her name, and added that she was acquainted with the Turner sisters and others who had been told they would benefit under Josiah Crowley's will.

"My dad—the lawyer Carson Drew—and I are working on the case. We believe there might have been a later will than the one presented by Mr. Topham, and we'd like to find it."

"And you came to see if William and I could give you a clue?" Fred's bright blue eyes sparkled boyishly.

"That's right, Mr. Mathews. Also, did Mr. Crowley ever tell you he was going to leave you some money?"

"Indeed he did."

At this moment another man came from the house and Fred introduced him as his brother William. Both were tall, spare, and strong-muscled. Though their hair was gray, the men's faces were youthful and unwrinkled.

"Let's sit down under the tree here and discuss this," Fred suggested, leading the way to a group of rustic chairs. He told William of Nancy's request, then asked him, "Did Cousin Josiah ever give you any idea he'd made a will in which we were not beneficiaries?"

"No. I thought one would come to light when he died. To tell the truth, Miss Drew, Fred and I were thunderstruck at the will which left everything to the Tophams. That wasn't what Cousin Josiah led us to believe."

"It certainly wasn't," Fred spoke up. "But I guess William and I counted our chickens before they were hatched. We just about make ends meet here with our small fruit farm. Help and equipment cost such a lot. One thing we've always wanted to do, but couldn't afford, was to travel. We thought we'd use the money from Cousin Josiah to do that."

"But our dream bubble burst," said William. "No trips for us."

Nancy smiled. "Don't give up hope yet. Dad and I haven't."

She was disappointed that the brothers could offer her no clues about a place to look for another will. A little while later she left the farm and returned home.

"No new evidence," she told her father. "Let's hope Mrs. Abby Rowen has some!"

Early the next morning she set off for the elderly

woman's home, and reached her destination by asking directions of people living along West Lake Road.

"This must be Abby Rowen's house," Nancy told herself. "It fits the description."

She climbed out of her car and stood before the one-story frame building which was badly in need of paint and repair. The yard around it was overgrown with weeds, and the picket fence enclosing the cottage sagged dejectedly.

"The place looks deserted," Nancy mused. "But I'll see if Mrs. Rowen is at home."

Nancy made her way up the scraggly path to the house and rapped on the front door. There was no response. After a moment, she knocked again.

This time a muffled voice called, "Who's there? If you're a peddler, I don't want anything."

"I'm not selling anything," Nancy called out reassuringly. "Won't you let me in, please?"

There was a long silence, then the quavering voice replied, "I can't open the door. I've hurt myself and can't walk."

Nancy hesitated an instant before pushing open the door. As she stepped into the dreary living room, she saw a frail figure on the couch. Abby Rowen lay huddled under an old shawl, her withered face drawn with pain.

"I am Nancy Drew and I've come to help you, Mrs. Rowen."

The old lady turned her head and regarded Nancy with a stare of wonder.

"You've come to help me?" she repeated unbelievingly. "I didn't think anyone would ever bother about old Abby again."

"Here, let me arrange the pillows for you." Gently Nancy moved the old woman into a more comfortable position.

"Yesterday I fell down the cellar stairs," Mrs. Rowen explained. "I hurt my hip and sprained my ankle."

"Haven't you had a doctor?" Nancy asked in astonishment.

"No." Abby Rowen sighed. "Not a soul has been here and I couldn't get in touch with anybody. I have no telephone."

"Can you walk at all?" Nancy asked.

"A little."

"Then your hip isn't broken," Nancy said in relief. "Let me see your ankle. Oh my, it is swollen! I'll bandage it for you."

"There's a clean cloth in the closet in the kitchen," Abby told her. "I haven't any regular bandage."

"You really should have a doctor," Nancy remarked. "Let me drive you to one."

"I can't afford it," the old woman murmured. "My pension check hasn't come, and it's too small, anyway."

"Let me pay the doctor," Nancy offered.

Abby Rowen shook her head stubbornly. "I'll not take charity. I'd rather die first."

"Well, if you insist upon not having a doctor, I'm going to the nearest drugstore and get some bandaging and a few other things," Nancy told her. "But before I go, I'll make you a cup of tea."

"There's no tea in the house."

"Then I'll get a box. What else do you need?"

"I need 'most everything, but I can't afford anything right now. You might get me some tea and a loaf of bread. That's enough. You'll find the money in a jar in the cupboard. It's not very much, but it's all I have."

"I'll be back in a few minutes," Nancy promised.

She stopped in the kitchen long enough to examine the cupboards. With the exception of a little flour and sugar and a can of soup, there appeared to be nothing in the house to eat. Nancy found that the money jar contained less than five dollars.

"I'll not take any of it," she decided.

Quietly the young sleuth slipped out the back door. She drove quickly to the nearest store and ordered a stock of groceries. Then she stopped at a drugstore and purchased bandages and liniment.

Reaching the cottage, she carried the supplies inside and adeptly set about making Abby Rowen more comfortable. She bathed the swollen ankle and bound it neatly with the antiseptic bandage.

"It feels better already," Mrs. Rowen told her gratefully. "I don't know what would have happened to me if you hadn't come."

"Oh, someone would have dropped in," said Nancy cheerfully. She went to the kitchen and in a short while prepared tea and a light lunch for the elderly woman.

As Abby Rowen ate the nourishing meal, Nancy was gratified to observe that almost immediately her patient became more cheerful and seemed to gain strength. She sat up on the couch and appeared eager to talk with Nancy.

"There aren't many folks willing to come in and help an old lady. If Josiah Crowley had lived, things would have been different," she declared. "I could have paid someone to look after me."

"It's strange that he didn't provide for you in his will," Nancy replied quietly.

She did not wish to excite the woman by telling her real mission. Yet Nancy hoped that she might lead her tactfully into a discussion of Josiah Crowley's affairs without raising hopes which might never be realized.

"It's my opinion that Josiah did provide for me," Mrs. Rowen returned emphatically. "Many a time he said to me, 'Abby, you'll never need to worry. When I'm gone you'll be well taken care of by my will.'"

"And then everything was left to the Tophams," Nancy encouraged her to proceed.

"That was according to the first will," Abby Rowen stated.

"You mean there was another will?" Nancy inquired eagerly.

"Of course. Why, I saw that will with my own eyes!"

"You saw it!" Nancy gasped.

The old woman nodded gravely. "Mind, I didn't see what was in the will. One day Josiah came to call and give me some money. Right off I noticed he had a bunch of papers in his hand. 'Abby,' he said, 'I've made a new will. I didn't bother with a lawyer. I wrote it myself.'"

"How long ago was that?" Nancy asked quickly.

"Let me see." Abby Rowen frowned thoughtfully. "I can't remember the exact date. It was this past spring. Anyway, Josiah hinted that he'd done well by me. 'But, Josiah,' I said, 'are you sure it's legal to write it yourself?' 'Of course it is,' he said. 'A lawyer told me it was all right, just so long as I wrote it myself and signed it. But I did have it witnessed.'"

"Do you know who witnessed the will?" Nancy broke in.

"No. He didn't say."

"Haven't you any idea what became of the will?" Nancy asked hopefully.

"Well, I remember Josiah did say something about putting it where nobody could get it unless they had legal authority. But I really don't know what became of it."

"Are you certain that was all Mr. Crowley said?" Nancy inquired gently. She recalled the Turners saying that Abby had become forgetful.

The elderly woman shook her head and sighed. "Many a night I've lain awake trying to think what else he did say about where he would put the will. I just can't recollect."

"Try to think!" Nancy begged.

"I can't remember," Abby Rowen murmured hopelessly. "I've tried and tried." She leaned against the cushions and closed her eyes, as though the effort had exhausted her.

At that very moment the clock on the mantel chimed twelve. Abby's eyes fluttered open and an odd expression passed over her face.

For an instant she stared straight before her, then slowly turned her head and fastened her eyes on the clock.

CHAPTER IX

Helpful Disclosures

Nancy watched Abby Rowen intently as the mantel clock finished striking. The elderly woman's lips had begun to move.

"The clock!" she whispered. "That was it! The clock!"

Nancy gripped the arms of her chair in excitement. "Josiah Crowley hid the will in a clock?" she prompted.

"No—no, it wasn't that," Abby murmured, sighing again. "I know Josiah said something about a clock, but whatever it was has slipped my mind."

Silence descended over the room. Nancy was wondering what connection the timepiece could have with the missing will. Mrs. Rowen was staring at the clock, evidently still trying to probe her memory.

Suddenly she gave a low cry. "There! It came to me just like that!"

"What, Mrs. Rowen?" Nancy urged quietly, lest she startle the old woman into forgetfulness.

"A notebook!" Abby exclaimed triumphantly.

Nancy's heart gave a leap, but she forced herself to say calmly, "Please tell me more about this notebook."

"Well, one day not long before he passed away, Josiah said to me, 'Abby, after I'm dead, if my last will isn't found, you can learn about it in this little book of mine.'"

"Do you know what became of the notebook, Mrs. Rowen?"

"Oh dearie me! There goes my memory again. No, I don't."

Although baffled, Nancy felt a growing conviction that the whereabouts of the Crowley will was definitely tied up with a clock of some kind. But, she pondered, why did the striking of the mantel clock remind Abby Rowen of the notebook?

Impulsively Nancy got up and went over to the mantel. She looked inside the glass front and in the back. There were no papers inside.

Returning to her chair, Nancy asked the elderly woman, "What became of the furnishings of the Crowley home when he gave it up?"

"The Tophams got 'most everything."

"There must have been a family clock," Nancy mused, half to herself.

"A family clock?" Abby repeated. "Oh, yes, there was a clock."

"Can you describe it?"

"It was just an ordinary mantel type, something like mine—tall, with a square face," the woman told Nancy. "Only Josiah's was fancier. Had some kind of a moon on top."

"What became of the clock?" Nancy questioned.

"I suppose the Tophams got it, too."

At last Nancy, sure she had done all she could for Abby, and that she had learned as much as possible for the present, rose to depart. After saying good-by, she stopped at a neighboring house and asked the occupants to look in occasionally on the ailing woman.

"I think maybe one of the county's visiting nurses should see Mrs. Rowen," she suggested.

"I'll phone the agency," the neighbor offered. "Meanwhile, I'll go over myself. I'm so sorry I didn't know about Mrs. Rowen."

As Nancy drove toward River Heights, she jubilantly reviewed the new facts in the case. "Now, if I can only locate Mr. Crowley's notebook—or clock—or both!"

Nancy's brow knit in concentration. How would she go about tracking down the old timepiece?

"I guess," she concluded, "if the Tophams *do* have the clock, I'll have to pay them a visit!"

While she did not relish the idea of calling on

the unpleasant family, Nancy was determined to pursue every possible clue. "I can just see Ada's and Isabel's expressions when I appear at their front door," Nancy thought wryly. "Well, I'll think of some excuse to see them."

She was still mulling over the problem when she pulled into the driveway of her home and heard a familiar voice calling her name.

"Why, Helen Corning!" exclaimed Nancy, as a slim, attractive school friend of hers ran up. "I haven't seen you for days."

"I've been busy lately," Helen explained, "trying to sell six tickets for a charity ball. But I haven't had much luck. Would you like a couple?"

A sudden idea flashed into Nancy's mind at her friend's words. "Helen," she said excitedly, "I'll buy two of your tickets and sell the rest for you."

The other girl stared in astonishment. "Why, that's a wonderful offer, Nance. But—"

Nancy's eyes danced. "I know you think I've lost my mind. I really mean it, though. Please let me take the tickets! I can't tell you my reasons yet—except my cause is a worthy one."

Helen, looking relieved but bewildered, handed over the tickets. "This is really a break for me," she said. "Now I can leave for my aunt's Camp Avondale this evening as I'd hoped. It's at Moon Lake. I thought I'd never get off, with those tickets unsold!"

Nancy smiled ''Have a grand time, Helen,'' she said.

"How about coming along? It's not expensive and there's room for lots more girls. We'd have loads of fun."

"I'd love to," Nancy replied, "but right now I can't get away."

"Maybe you can make it later," Helen suggested. "If so, just zip on up. I'll be there for two weeks before the regular summer camp opens."

The two friends chatted a little longer, then said good-by. Nancy put the car away, then walked slowly toward her house, looking meditatively at the charity tickets in her hand.

"These are to be my passport to the Tophams' stronghold!"

It was the following afternoon when Nancy approached the large pretentious house belonging to the Tophams.

Bracing herself for what she realized would be a trying interview, Nancy mounted the steps and rang the doorbell. "Here goes," she thought. "I must be subtle in this maneuver to keep from arousing the Tophams' suspicions!"

At that moment a maid opened the door, and with a condescending look, waited for Nancy to state her mission.

"Will you please tell Mrs. Topham that Nancy Drew is calling?" she requested. "I'm selling tickets for a charity dance. It's one of the most important functions of the year in River Heights," Nancy added impressively.

It seemed ages to the young sleuth before the maid returned and said that "Madame" would see her. Nancy was ushered into the living room, which was so bizarre in its decor she was startled.

"Such an expensive hodge-podge!" Nancy observed to herself, sitting down. She glanced at the pink carpet—which to her clashed with the red window draperies—and at an indiscriminate assortment of period furniture mixed with modern.

A haughty voice interrupted her thoughts. "Well, what do you want, Nancy?" Mrs. Topham had sailed grandly into the room and seated herself opposite Nancy.

"I'm selling—" Nancy began pleasantly.

"Oh, if you're selling things I'm not interested," the woman broke in rudely. "I can't be handing out money to every solicitor who comes along."

With difficulty Nancy suppressed an angry retort to the cutting remark. "Mrs. Topham," she said evenly, "perhaps your maid didn't make it clear. I am selling tickets to a charity ball which will be one of the loveliest affairs in River Heights this year."

"Oh!" A slight change came over Mrs. Topham's face. Nancy sensed that her words had struck a responsive chord. The woman was well known for her aspirations to be accepted by the best families in River Heights. "Well—"

To Nancy's dismay Mrs. Topham's response was cut off by the arrival of Ada and Isabel. The sisters entered the room, but did not at first notice Nancy's presence. They were intently carrying on a disgruntled conversation.

"Really!" Ada was complaining. "I'm positive that woman snubbed us deliberately."

Then she and Isabel caught sight of Nancy and stopped short. They stared coldly at the visitor.

"What are *you* doing here?" Isabel asked with a patronizing air.

Mrs. Topham answered her daughter's question. "Nancy is selling tickets to a charity dance, dear. It's to be a very important affair and I think it will be—er—beneficial—for us to be present."

Isabel tossed her head disdainfully. "Don't waste your money, Mother."

"Isabel's right," Ada chimed in. "We don't want to go to a ball just anybody can go to. We only attend the most exclusive affairs."

"Absolutely," Isabel declared in her haughtiest tone. "After all, Ada and I are very particular about the people we choose to meet."

Mrs. Topham hesitated, evidently influenced by her daughters' argument. Nancy's heart sank, and she feared her cause was lost. She fully realized that Ada and Isabel would stay away from the dance just to spite her.

As she debated what her next move should be, Richard Topham walked into the living room.

He was a thin man, with sparse graying hair. His manner was rather nervous. Mrs. Topham perfunctorily introduced Nancy to her husband.

"I gather you have some tickets to dispose of, Miss Drew," he said without ceremony. "How many?"

"Why, four," Nancy replied in some surprise.

"I'll take them all." Mr. Topham opened his wallet with a flourish and drew out a hundred-dollar bill. Here you are. Keep the change for your charity."

His daughters gasped and his wife exclaimed, "Richard! Have you lost your senses? All that money!"

"Listen," Mr. Topham retorted bluntly. "This donation will entitle us to have our names on the programs as patrons."

With this remark he slumped into a chair and buried himself in the financial section of the newspaper. His family stared at one another, but they knew that the matter was closed. They never dared disturb him when he was absorbed in the stock-market reports.

Nancy arose reluctantly. She still had not accomplished the real purpose of her visit, but she had no excuse for prolonging her stay. How could she find out about the Crowley clock? Was it the one on the mantelpiece?

"I must be going," she said. Then, looking at her wrist watch, she pretended that it had stopped and began to wind it. "What time is it, please?"

"There's a clock right in front of you—on the mantel," Ada said sharply.

Nancy looked at the timepiece. "So there is," she remarked casually. "Is it an heirloom, perhaps the old Crowley clock I've heard so much about?"

Mrs. Topham looked down her nose. "I should say not! This is a far more expensive one!"

Isabel also rose to Nancy's bait. "Cousin Josiah's old clock was a monstrosity. We wouldn't even have it cluttering up the attic!"

Nancy's hopes waned, but she asked quickly, "Oh, then you sold it?"

"No," Ada spoke up contemptuously. "Who'd give any money for that piece of junk? We sent it up to our bungalow at Moon Lake."

Moon Lake! The words hit Nancy like a thunderbolt. Not only had the Topham girl given Nancy the very information she sought, but Helen Corning's invitation to Camp Avondale provided a valid reason to visit the resort! Now if she could only figure out how to see the old clock!

As if Ada had read the visitor's thoughts, she said airily, "We have some really fine pieces up at the cottage, Nancy. If you ever get up that way, drop in to see them. The caretaker will show you around."

"Thank you. Thank you so much for everything," Nancy said, trying hard to conceal her excitement. As the door closed behind her, Nancy grinned in anticipation.

"What luck!" she told herself. "Moon Lake, here I come!"

CHAPTER X

Following a Clue

WITH soaring spirits, Nancy walked homeward. "I wonder," she thought, "how the Tophams will feel about Josiah Crowley's old clock if it costs them the inheritance they're counting on."

At dinner that night Nancy chatted with unusual animation, deciding not to tell of her exciting plans until after Hannah had served dessert.

Mr. Drew, however, sensed that big news was coming. "My dear," he said, laying a hand on his daughter's arm, "you look like the cat that swallowed the canary. What's the big scoop?"

Nancy giggled. "Oh, Dad. I can't keep any secrets from you." Then, as the table was cleared, the young sleuth told of her great stroke of luck. "And just think, Helen invited me to her aunt's camp!"

"Good," her father commented, smiling. "You

can combine business with pleasure, Nancy. Swimming and boating and fun with the girls will provide a much-needed vacation."

"May I start first thing in the morning?" his daughter asked.

"An excellent idea, Nancy. The change will do wonders for you. Go, by all means."

Hurriedly she packed a suitcase and the next morning was off to an early start.

Moon Lake was about a fifty-mile drive. One way to go was past the Hoover girls' farm and Nancy decided to stop there. As she approached the house, the young sleuth heard singing. It was coming from the barn.

"How beautiful!" Nancy thought, as the clear soprano voice went through a series of trills and flutelike scales.

In a moment the singer appeared and Nancy teasingly applauded. Allison's eyes danced. "Thanks. I was just trying to imitate some of the greats."

"You'll be great yourself one of these days," Nancy prophesied.

"Not unless I get some money to finance lessons," Allison said. "Any news, Nancy?"

"Sort of. I've had a little luck." At this moment Grace appeared and instantly invited Nancy to stay, but the young detective said she too had work to do. "I hope to have a good report for you soon," she added, and waved good-by.

Grace's face brightened and Allison declared cheerfully, "Then there's still hope? We are so lucky to have you as a friend, Nancy. Come see us again soon. Please."

Resuming her journey, Nancy soon branched off from the River Road and headed toward Moon Lake. As she drove along, her thoughts revolved constantly around the Crowley relatives and the Hoovers.

She sighed. "How different things would be for them now if Josiah Crowley hadn't been so secretive!"

Her reverie was ended by the sudden strange actions of her car. It kept veering to the left of the road in spite of her efforts to keep it in the middle. With foreboding, Nancy stopped and got out to make an inspection. As she had suspected, a rear tire was flat.

"Oh dear!" she murmured in disgust. "Such luck!"

Though Nancy was able to change a tire, she never relished the task. Quickly she took out the spare tire from the rear compartment, found the jack and lug wrench, and went to work. By the

time her job was completed, she was hot and a little breathless.

"Whew!" she exclaimed, as she started on her way again. "I'll be ready for a nice, cool swim in Moon Lake!"

It was after twelve o'clock when she came in sight of Camp Avondale, run by Helen's aunt. Through the tall trees Nancy caught a glimpse of cabins and tents. Beyond, the blue lake sparkled and glimmered in the sunlight.

As Nancy drove into the camp, a group of girls gathered about her car. Helen came running out of a cabin to greet her chum.

"Girls, it's Nancy Drew!" she exclaimed joyfully and made introductions. Nancy did not know any of the campers, but in no time they made her feel warmly welcome.

"Nancy," said Helen, "park your car back of the dining hall, then come have lunch."

"That sounds wonderful." Nancy laughed. "I'm nearly starved!"

First, she was escorted to the main building where she met Aunt Martha, the camp director, and registered.

"May she stay with me?" Helen asked.

"Certainly, dear. And I hope you have a splendid time, Nancy."

"I'm sure I shall, Aunt Martha."

As the two girls walked off Nancy told Helen

about selling the charity-dance tickets and gave her the money paid by Mr. Topham.

"He surely was generous!" Helen commented in surprise. Then she smiled wryly. "I have a feeling he did it more for social prestige than sympathy for the cause."

Nancy scarcely had time to deposit her suitcase under her cot and freshen up after the long ride when lunch was announced by the ringing of a bell. Campers hurried from all directions to the dining hall. The food was plain but appetizing and Nancy ate with zest.

The meal over, she was rushed from one activity to another. The girls insisted that she join them in a hike. Then came a cooling dip in the lake. Nancy enjoyed herself immensely, but the Crowley mystery was never far from her mind.

"I must find out where the Tophams' cottage is located," she reminded herself. "And next, manage to go there alone."

Nancy's opportunity to accomplish the first part of her quest came when Helen suggested about five o'clock, "How about going for a ride around the lake in the camp launch? There's just time before supper."

"Wonderful!" Nancy accepted readily. "By the way, can you see many of the summer cottages from the water?"

"Oh, yes. Lots of them."

Helen led her friend down to a small dock and with four other girls climbed into the launch, a medium-sized craft.

As one of the campers started the motor, Helen remarked, "It's always a relief to us when this engine starts. Once in a while it balks, but you never know when or where."

"Yes," spoke up a girl named Barby. "And when you're stuck this time of year, you're stuck. There are hardly any cottagers up here yet, so their boats are still in winter storage."

As the little launch turned out into the lake, Nancy was entranced with the beautiful sight before her. The delicate azure blue of the sky and the mellow gold of the late afternoon sun were reflected in the shimmering surface of the water.

"What a lovely scene for an oil painting!" she thought.

As they sped along, however, Nancy kept glancing at the cottages, intermingled with tall evergreen trees that bordered the shore line.

"The Tophams have a bungalow up here, haven't they?" she questioned casually.

"Yes, it's across the lake," Helen replied. "We'll come to it soon."

"Is anyone staying there now?"

"Oh, no, the cottage is closed. It's being looked after by Jeff Tucker, the caretaker. He's the tallest, skinniest man I've ever seen outside a circus."

"Is it hard to get to the place?"

"Not if you go by launch. But it's a long way if you take the road around the lake." Helen looked at her friend. "I didn't know you were particularly interested in the Tophams, Nancy."

"Oh, they're not friends of mine, as you know," Nancy returned hastily. "I was merely curious."

After a time, as the launch slowed down and chugged along close to shore, Helen pointed out a wide path through the woods. At the end of it stood a large, rambling white cottage.

"That's the Topham place," she said.

Trying not to appear too eager, Nancy looked intently at the bungalow. She made a quick mental note of its location.

"Tomorrow I'll visit that place and try to solve the mystery!" she told herself.

CHAPTER XI

An Unexpected Adventure

NANCY awoke the next morning to the fragrant odor of pines. Eager to start out for the Topham bungalow, she dressed quickly.

But in her plans she had reckoned without Helen Corning and her friends. From the moment breakfast was over, Nancy was swept into another whirlwind of activity by the campers of Avondale. The entire day passed without a chance for her to break away.

"Oh, Helen!" Nancy groaned as she tumbled into bed that night. "Tennis matches, canoe races, swimming, water skiing—it's been fun. But tomorrow I think I'll stay out of the activities."

Helen laughed gaily. "You'll change your mind after a sound sleep, Nancy. Wait and see."

For answer, Nancy murmured a sleepy good night. But even as she slipped into slumber, she vowed that in the morning she would not be deterred again from visiting the Tophams' summer place!

After breakfast the next day, Nancy stood firm in her resolve. When Helen urged her to accompany the girls on an all-day hike, Nancy shook her head.

"Thanks a lot, but please excuse me today, Helen."

Normally Nancy would have loved going on such a hike. But she had to achieve her plan of sleuthing. Helen, though disappointed, heeded her friend's plea and trudged off with the other campers into the woods.

As soon as they were out of sight, Nancy leaped into action. After obtaining Aunt Martha's permission to use the launch, she hurried down to the dock. Nancy had frequently handled motorboats and was confident she could manage this one.

"Now. Full speed ahead for the Tophams'!"

To her delight the motor started immediately, and Nancy steered out into the lake. As the launch cut through the water, a cool spray blew into her face. The young sleuth felt a thrill of excitement as she guided the craft toward her destination which might hold a solution to the mystery.

"If only the Tophams' caretaker will let me in when I get there!" she thought.

Nancy's heart beat somewhat faster as she neared her goal. But all of a sudden there was a sputter from the engine. The next instant, to Nancy's utter dismay, the motor gave one long wheeze and died.

"Oh!" she cried aloud.

Nancy knew that the tank held plenty of fuel, for she had checked this before departing. A moment later she recalled Helen's remark about the engine becoming balky at times.

With a sigh of impatience at the unexpected delay, Nancy examined the motor. For over an hour she worked on it, trying every adjustment she could think of. But her efforts were useless. There was not a sound of response from the motor.

"What miserable luck!" she said aloud. "Of all days for the motor to conk out! This means I won't get to the Topham cottage after all!"

For a moment Nancy was tempted to swim ashore. To be so close to the bungalow and not be able to reach it was tantalizing. But she resisted the impulse; she could not leave the boat stranded—it would drift off and she would be responsible.

"I'll just have to wait for a passing boat to rescue me," Nancy decided.

But fate was against her. The hours dragged by and not another craft appeared in sight. Nancy became increasingly uncomfortable as the hot sun beat down on her. Also, she was growing weak from hunger.

"And worst of all," Nancy thought gloomily,

"another whole day is being wasted. I want to get to the bottom of this mystery!"

To occupy her mind, Nancy concentrated once more on the motor. Determinedly she bent over the engine. It was not until the sun sank low in the sky that she sat up and drew a long breath.

"There!" she declared. "I've done everything. If it doesn't start now, it never will."

To her relief and astonishment, it responded with a steady roar as if nothing had ever gone wrong!

Nancy lost no time in heading back toward camp. She dared not attempt to visit the bungalow, since it would be dark very soon.

When finally she eased up to the dock, Nancy saw Helen and her friends awaiting her. They greeted her with delight.

"We were just going to send out a search party for you!" Helen exclaimed. She stopped abruptly and stared at her friend. "You're sunburned and covered with grease! What happened?"

Nancy laughed. "I had an extended sun bath." Then she gave a lighthearted account of her mishap as the campers trooped back to their cabins. When Helen learned that Nancy had had nothing to eat since breakfast, she went to the kitchen and brought back some food.

The following morning the young sleuth decided on her next move. Directly after breakfast she began packing.

When Helen entered the cabin she exclaimed in amazement, "Why, Nancy Drew! You're not leaving camp already!"

"I'm afraid I'll have to, Helen. Right after lunch. I may be back but I'm not sure, so I'd better take my bag with me."

"Don't you like it here?"

"Of course!" Nancy assured her. "I've had a wonderful time. It's just that there's something very important I must attend to at once."

Helen looked at her friend searchingly, then grinned. "Nancy Drew, you're working on some mystery with your father!"

"Well, sort of," Nancy admitted. "But I'll try to get back. Okay?"

"Oh, please do," Helen begged.

Nancy went to the office to pay Aunt Martha and explain her hasty departure. After lunch she set off in her car to a chorus of farewells from the campers, who sadly watched her depart.

She headed the car toward the end of the lake, then took the dirt road leading to the Topham cottage. Soon she came to a fork in the woods.

"Now, which way shall I turn for the bungalow?" she wondered. After a moment's hesitation, Nancy calculated that she should turn left toward the water and did so.

The going was rather rough due to ruts in the road. Two of them, deeper than the others, apparently had been made by a heavy truck.

"The tracks appear fresh," Nancy mused.

As she drove along, the young sleuth noticed a number of summer cottages. Most of them were still boarded up, since it was early in the season. As she gazed at one of them, the steering wheel was nearly wrenched from her hand by a crooked rut. As Nancy turned the steering wheel, to bring the car back to the center of the narrow road, one hand accidentally touched the horn. It blared loudly in the still woods.

"That must have scared all the birds and animals." Nancy chuckled.

Around a bend in the road, she caught sight of a white bungalow ahead on the right side of the road.

There was no sign at the entrance to the driveway to indicate who the owner was, but a wooded path leading down to the lake looked like the one she had seen from the water.

"I think I'll walk down to the shore and look at the cottage from there," Nancy determined. "Then I'll know for sure if this is the place Helen pointed out."

Nancy parked at the edge of the road and got out. To her surprise, she observed that the truck's tire marks turned into the driveway. A second set of tracks indicated that the vehicle had backed out and gone on down the road.

"Delivering supplies for the summer, no doubt," Nancy told herself.

She went down the path to the water, then turned around to look at the cottage.

"It's the Tophams' all right," Nancy decided.

Instead of coming back by way of the path, she decided to take a short cut through the woods. With mounting anticipation of solving the Crowley mystery, she reached the road and hurried up the driveway.

"I hope the caretaker is here," she thought.

Nancy suddenly stopped short with a gasp of astonishment. "Why, the Tophams must be moving out!"

The front and side doors of the cottage stood wide open. Some of the furniture on the porch was overturned and various small household items were strewn along the driveway.

Nancy bent to examine some marks in the soft earth. She noted that several were boot prints, while others were long lines probably caused by dragging cartons and furniture across the lawn.

"That must have been a moving van's tracks I saw," Nancy told herself. "But the Tophams didn't say anything about moving." She frowned in puzzlement.

Her feeling persisted and grew strong as she walked up the steps of the cottage porch. Nancy knocked loudly on the opened door. No response. Nancy rapped again. Silence.

Where was Jeff Tucker, the caretaker? Why wasn't he on hand to keep an eye on the moving activities? An air of complete desertion hung over the place.

"There's something very strange about this," she thought.

Curious and puzzled, Nancy entered the living room. Again her eyes met a scene of disorder. Except for a few small pieces, the room was bare of furniture. Even the draperies had been pulled from their rods and all floor coverings were gone.

"Hm! Most of the furnishings have been taken out," Nancy thought. "I suppose the movers will be back for the other odds and ends."

She made a careful tour of the first floor. All but one room had been virtually emptied. This was a small study. As Nancy entered it, she noticed that the rug lay rolled up and tied, and some of the furniture had evidently been shifted in readiness for moving.

"Funny I didn't hear anything about the Tophams deciding to give up their cottage," she murmured. "And I must say those moving men were awfully careless—"

A vague suspicion that had been forming in the back of Nancy's mind now came into startling focus. "Those men may not be movers!" she burst out. "They may be thieves!"

At once Nancy thought of the dark-gray van which had stopped at the Turners. "Those men may be the same ones who robbed them!"

That would explain, Nancy thought fearfully,

the evidences of the truck's hasty departure. "Probably the thieves were scared away when I sounded my horn!"

Nancy glanced about uneasily. What if the men were still nearby, watching for a chance to return and pick up the remaining valuables? The realization that she was alone, some distance from the nearest house, swept over her. A tingling sensation crept up Nancy's spine.

But resolutely she shook off her nervousness. "At least I must see if the Crowley clock is still here," Nancy reminded herself, and then went through the bungalow again.

She found no trace of the timepiece, however. "I guess the thieves took that too," Nancy concluded. "I'd better report this robbery to the police right now." She looked about for a phone but there was none. "I'll have to drive to the nearest State Police headquarters."

Nancy started toward the front door. Passing a window, she glanced out, then paused in sheer fright. A man, wearing a cap pulled low over his eyes, was stalking up the driveway toward the cottage. He was not tall and slender like the caretaker. This stranger was rather short and heavyset.

"This man fits the Turners' description! He must be one of the thieves who stole the silver heirlooms!" Nancy thought wildly.

CHAPTER XII

A Desperate Situation

FOR A moment Nancy stood frozen to the spot, positive that the man who was coming to the Topham cottage was one of the thieves.

But she hesitated only an instant. Then she turned and ran back into the study. Too late she realized that she had trapped herself, for this room had no other door.

Nancy started back toward the living room. But before she had taken half a dozen steps she knew that escape had been cut off from that direction. The man had reached the porch steps.

"It won't do a bit of good to talk to him," she reasoned. "I'll hide, and when he leaves, I'll follow him in my car and report him to the police!"

Frantically the young sleuth glanced about for a hiding place. A closet offered the only possible refuge. She scurried inside and closed the door.

Nancy was not a second too soon. She had scarcely shut the door when she heard the tread of the man's heavy shoes on the floor just outside. Peeping cautiously through a tiny crack in the door, she saw the heavy-set man come into the study. His face wore a cruel expression.

As he turned toward the closet where she huddled, Nancy hardly dared to breathe, lest her presence be detected. Apparently the man noticed nothing amiss, because his eyes rested only casually on the door.

Nancy's hiding place was anything but comfortable. It was dark and musty, and old clothing hung from nails on the walls. As dust assailed her nostrils, she held a handkerchief to her face.

"If I sneeze he'll surely find me," she told herself.

She felt around and once came close to ripping her hand on a sharp nail. Then she came upon something soft on a shelf and imagined it was a sleeping cat. She drew back, then touched it more cautiously.

"Only an old fur cap," she told herself in disgust. "O-oo, now I feel like sneezing more than ever!"

She held one hand over her mouth hard and waited in agony. But presently the desire to sneeze passed and Nancy breathed more freely.

When she dared to peep out through the crack a second time, she saw that two other rough-looking men had come into the room. One was short and stout, the other taller. Nancy was sure that neither of these two men was the caretaker, because Helen Corning had mentioned that the man was skinny.

The heavy-set man who had come in first seemed to be the leader, for he proceeded to issue orders. "Get a move on!" he growled. "We haven't got all day unless we want to be caught. That girl you saw, Jake, may be back any time from the shore. And she just might get snoopy."

The man addressed as Jake scowled. "What's the matter with you, Sid? Going chicken? If that girl comes around, we'll just give her a smooth story and send her on her way."

"Cut out the yaking," said Sid. "Parky, you and Jake take that desk out of here."

There was no doubt now in Nancy's mind. She was trapped by a clever gang of thieves! She could only continue to watch and listen helplessly from her hiding place.

The two men lifted the heavy piece of furniture and started with it to the door. But they did not move swiftly enough to satisfy the leader, and he berated them savagely.

Jake turned on him. "If you're in such a hurry, why don't you bring the van back to the driveway, instead of leaving it hidden on that road in the woods?"

"And have someone driving past here see us!" sneered the leader. "Now get going!"

Little by little the men stripped the room of

everything valuable. Nancy was given no opportunity to escape. Sid remained in the room while the others made several trips to the van.

"Well, I guess we have all the stuff that's worth anything now," Sid muttered at last.

He turned to follow his companions, who already had left the room, but in the doorway he paused for a final careful survey of the room.

At that same moment Nancy felt an uncontrollable urge to sneeze. She tried to muffle the sound, but to no avail.

The thief wheeled about. "Hey! What—"

Walking directly to the closet, he flung open the door. Instantly he spotted Nancy and angrily jerked her out.

"Spying on us, eh?" he snarled.

Nancy faced the man defiantly. "I wasn't spying on anyone."

"Then what were you doing in that closet?" the thief demanded, his eyes narrowing to slits.

"I came to see the caretaker."

"Looking for him in a funny place, ain't you?" the man sneered.

Nancy realized that she was in a desperate situation. But she steeled herself not to show any of her inward fears.

"I must keep calm," she told herself firmly. Aloud, she explained coolly, "I heard someone coming and I just felt a bit nervous."

"Well, you're going to be a lot more nervous,"

the man said threateningly. "This will be the last time you'll ever stick your nose in business that doesn't concern you!"

A fresh wave of fright swept over Nancy, but resolutely she held on to her courage. "You have no right to be here, helping yourself to the Tophams' furniture!" she retorted. "You should be turned over to the police!"

"Well, you'll never get the chance to do it." The ringleader laughed loudly. "You'll wish you'd never come snoopin' around here. I'll give you the same treatment the caretaker got."

"The caretaker!" Nancy gasped in horror. "What have you done to him?"

"You'll find out in good time."

Nancy gave a sudden agile twist, darted past the man, and raced for the door. The thief gave a cry of rage, and in one long leap overtook her. He caught Nancy roughly by the arm.

"Think you're smart, eh?" he snarled. "Well, I'm smarter!"

Nancy struggled to get away. She twisted and squirmed, kicked and clawed. But she was helpless in the viselike grip of the powerful man.

"Let me go!" Nancy cried, struggling harder. "Let me go!"

Sid, ignoring her pleas, half dragged her across the room. Opening the closet door, he flung her inside.

Nancy heard a key turn.

"Now you can spy all you want!" Sid sneered. "But to make sure nobody'll let you out, I'll just take this key along."

When Nancy could no longer hear the tramp of his heavy boots she was sure Sid had left the house. For a moment a feeling of great relief engulfed her.

But the next instant Nancy's heart gave a leap. As she heard the muffled roar of the van starting up in the distance, a horrifying realization gripped her.

"They've left me here to—to starve!" she thought frantically.

CHAPTER XIII

The Frustrating Wait

AT FIRST Nancy was too frightened to think logically. She beat upon the door with her fists, but the heavy oak panels would not give way.

"Help! Help!" she screamed.

At last, exhausted by her efforts to force the door open, she sank down on the floor. The house was as silent as a tomb. Bad as her predicament was, Nancy felt thankful that enough air seeped into the closet to permit normal breathing.

Although she had little hope that there was anyone within miles of the cottage, Nancy got to her feet, raised her voice, and again shouted for help. Her cries echoed through the empty house and seemed to mock her.

"Oh, why didn't I have enough sense to tell Helen where I was going?" she berated herself miserably. "The girls at camp will never dream that I came here."

Then Nancy remembered mournfully that her father thought she intended to remain at Camp Avondale for a week! He would not become alarmed over her absence until it was too late.

"Someone may find my car at the side of the road," Nancy reasoned, "but it isn't very likely. Few persons pass this way so early in the season."

She wondered, with a shudder, what had become of Jeff Tucker. The thief called Sid had hinted that the caretaker had received the same treatment as Nancy. If he was locked up somewhere, she could expect no aid from him.

"Those thieves will get so far away that even if I could get out of here, I'd be too late."

As the full significance of the situation dawned upon Nancy, panic again took possession of her. In a desperate attempt to break down the door, she threw her weight against it again and again. She pounded on the panels until her fingers were bruised and bleeding. At last she sank down again on the floor to rest and tried to force herself to reason calmly.

"I'm only wasting my strength this way. I *must* try to think logically."

Nancy recalled that it was sometimes possible to pick a lock with a wire. She removed a bobby pin from her hair, opened it, and began to work at the lock. But in the darkness she could not see and made no progress. After fifteen minutes she gave up the task in disgust.

"It's no use," she decided dejectedly. "I—I guess I'm in here for good."

She began to think of her father, of Hannah Gruen, of Helen Corning, and other dear friends. Would she ever see them again? As despondency claimed Nancy, she was dangerously near tears.

"This will never do," she reprimanded herself sternly. "I must keep my head and try to think of some way to escape."

The trapped girl began to rummage in the closet, hoping that by some lucky chance she might find a tool which would help her force the lock of the door. Nancy searched carefully through the pockets of every garment which hung from the hooks. She groped over every inch of the floor.

She found nothing useful, however, and the cloud of dust which she had stirred up made breathing more difficult than before. The closet had become uncomfortably warm by this time. Longingly she thought of the fresh air and cool lake water from which she was closed off.

Then, unexpectedly, Nancy's hand struck something hard. Quickly investigating with her fingers, she discovered a wooden rod suspended high overhead. It was fastened to either side wall and ran the length of the closet. Evidently it had once been used for dress and coat hangers.

"I might be able to use that rod to break out a panel of the door," Nancy thought hopefully. "It feels strong and it's about the right size."

She tugged at the rod with all her might. When it did not budge, she swung herself back and forth on it. At last, amid the cracking of plaster, one side gave way. Another hard jerk brought the rod down.

To Nancy's bitter. disappointment, she found that unfortunately the rod was too long to use as a ram in the cramped space. But after further examination, she discovered that it had pointed ends.

"I might use this rod as a wedge in the crack," she thought hopefully.

The young sleuth inserted one end in the space between the hinges and the door, and threw all her weight against the rod. At first the door did not move in the slightest.

"That old Greek scientist, Archimedes, didn't know what he was talking about when he said the world could be moved with a lever," Nancy murmured. "I'd like to see him move this door!"

As she applied steady pressure to the rod a second time, she saw that the hinges were beginning to give. Encouraged, Nancy again pushed full force on the "lever."

"It's coming!" she cried.

Once more she threw her weight against the rod. A hinge tore from the casing and the door sagged. It was now easy to insert the wedge, and Nancy joyously realized that success would soon be hers. With renewed strength she continued her efforts.

Then, just as another hinge gave way, she was startled to hear footsteps. Someone came running into the study, and a heavy body hurled itself against the door of the closet.

For a moment Nancy was stunned. Could this be one of the thieves who had heard the noise she had made and had returned to make sure that she did not escape? She discarded the theory quickly. Surely the three men would want to get far away as quickly as possible. But who was this new-comer? One of the Tophams?

"So, one o' you ornery robbers got yourself locked up, did you?" came an indignant male voice. "That'll teach you to try puttin' one over on old Jeff Tucker. You won't be doin' any more pil-ferin'. I got you surrounded."

The caretaker! Nancy heaved a sigh of fervent relief. "Let me out!" she pleaded. "I'm not one of the thieves! If you'll only let me out of here, I'll explain everything!"

There was silence for a moment. Then the voice on the other side of the door said dubiously, "Say, you aimin' to throw me off, imitatin' a lady's voice? Well, it won't do you any good! No, sir. Old Jeff Tucker's not gettin' fooled again!"

Nancy decided to convince the man beyond doubt. She gave a long, loud feminine scream.

"All right, *all right,* ma'am. I believe you! No man could make that racket. This way out, lady!"

Expectantly Nancy waited. But the door did not open. Then she heard to her dismay:

"If that ain't the limit. The key's gone and I've left my ring o' extra keys somewhere. It's not in my pockets."

Nancy groaned. "Oh, Mr. Tucker, you must find it. Have you looked in every one of your pockets? Please hurry and get me out."

"Hold on, ma'am," the caretaker said soothingly. "I'll just check again."

Nancy was beginning to think she would still have to break down the door, when she heard Jeff Tucker exclaim, "Found it! You were right, ma'am. Key was in my back pocket all the time. It—"

"*Please* open the door!" Nancy broke in desperately.

A key turned in the lock and the bolt clicked. Joyfully Nancy pushed the door open and stepped out. For a moment the bright sunlight in the room almost blinded her. When her vision adjusted, she saw a very tall, thin, elderly man in blue shirt and overalls. He stared at her with concern and amazement.

"Mr. Tucker," she explained quickly, "I'm Nancy Drew. I was here looking for you when those awful thieves came and locked me in the closet." She paused and gazed at the caretaker. "I'm glad to see that you're all right. Their leader told me they'd locked you up too." She then asked the elderly man to tell his story.

Jeff Tucker seemed embarrassed as he began to speak. "I was plain hornswoggled by those critters, Miss Drew. They pulled up here in a movin' van, and told me I'd better get after some trespassers they'd seen nearby. So," the elderly man went on with a sigh, "I believed 'em. One of the men went with me down to the lake and locked me in a shed. I just got out." He shook his head sadly. "And all this time they was robbin' the place. Guess I'll be fired."

Secretly Nancy was inclined to agree, knowing the Tophams. But aloud she said reassuringly:

"Don't worry, Mr. Tucker. We'll report this robbery to the State Police immediately. Perhaps the troopers can catch the thieves before they get rid of the stolen furniture."

The caretaker looked somewhat relieved. "And I can sure give a good description o' those crooks. I'd never forget their ugly faces!"

"Fine," said Nancy. A sudden thought struck her. "Oh, before we go, Mr. Tucker, tell me, was there an old clock in this house? A tall, square-faced mantel clock?"

Jeff Tucker's bright blue eyes squinted. "Mantel clock? Hm. Why, sure enough!" He pointed to the mantel over the living-room fireplace. "Sat right up there. Got so used to seein' it, I couldn't remember for a minute. Don't know how come they took that too. Never thought it was worth much. The Tophams never bothered windin' the thing."

Nancy's pulse quickened. Knowing that the clock had been stolen, she was more eager than ever to have the thieves apprehended. She urged Jeff Tucker to hurry out to her car.

"Where's the nearest State Police headquarters?" she asked him as they climbed into the convertible.

"There's none till you get to Melborne, Miss Drew."

"We'll hurry."

Nancy headed as fast as possible for the highway. Would she succeed in heading off the thieves and recovering the old Crowley clock, so she could learn its secret?

CHAPTER XIV

A Tense Chase

"WHICH way is Melborne?" Nancy asked the caretaker when they reached the highway.

"Down there." He pointed.

"That's the direction the thieves took," Nancy told him, noting the dust and tire marks which revealed the van's exit onto the highway. "But," she added, glancing at the dashboard clock, "they're probably too far away by this time for us to catch them."

"Yes, ding it," Jeff muttered.

Nancy drove as rapidly as the law permitted toward Melborne. All the while, Jeff Tucker peered from one side of the road to the other.

"Those rascal thieves might just have nerve enough to stop an' count their loot," he said to Nancy. "So I'm keepin' a sharp eye peeled."

Nancy smiled in spite of the gravity of the situation. "Maybe," she replied. "Though I doubt that those men would be so reckless."

"Oh, I don't mean out in plain sight. They might have pulled off the road, back o' some o' these closed-up summer places."

"We'll watch for their tire marks on any dirt side road," the young sleuth said.

Jeff became so absorbed in looking for the van's tire marks that he never asked Nancy why she had come to see him at the Topham house.

"Those fake movers," he said, as they neared the outskirts of Melborne. "I wonder how far they went."

Nancy did not reply until they came to a crossroad, then she pointed. "They turned north here on this dirt road. How much farther is it to Melborne?"

"Only a mile."

As they came into the little town, Nancy asked her companion, "Which way to State Police headquarters?"

"Go right down Central Avenue to Maple Street. Turn left, and there it is."

Reaching headquarters, Nancy parked the car and hopped out. Jeff Tucker followed as she walked briskly into the office.

"I want to report a robbery," she told the desk sergeant after identifying herself.

For a moment the officer, taken aback, looked in astonishment at Nancy. "You've been robbed?" he asked. "In *our* town?"

"No, no!" Nancy cried out. She then gave a

Nancy reported what had taken place at the
Tophams' cottage

quick but complete resume of what had taken place at the Tophams' cottage. Jeff Tucker added his account.

The police officer needed no further urging. Immediately he summoned four men and issued orders. "Now," he said, turning to Nancy, "have you any idea which road the thieves took?"

"Yes, Officer. When we passed the road crossing a mile outside of town, I saw their truck tracks on the dirt road leading north. I'll be glad to show you."

"Good. Lead the way. But first I'll send out a general alarm."

"Hurry!" Nancy begged as she started out. "Those thieves have at least an hour's head start!"

Jeff Tucker had been advised to return to his home. Accordingly he telephoned his son to come and pick him up in his car.

"Good luck!" he called, as the others pulled away. "I sure don't know how I'm goin' to break this to the Tophams."

Nancy was sorry for him, but she felt a thrill of excitement as she proceeded up the street, the police car following close behind.

Beyond the town, Nancy chose the road which she felt certain the thieves had used. The two cars sped along until Nancy unexpectedly came to a fork. Both branches were paved and no tire marks were visible. Nancy stopped. The police car pulled up alongside.

"What's the matter?" asked the officer in charge, whose name was Elton.

"I'm not sure which way to go now."

The policemen sprang from their automobile and began to examine the road. Officer Elton said that if a moving van had passed that way, its tire marks had been obliterated by other vehicles. It was impossible to tell which route the thieves had traveled.

"It'll be strictly guesswork from here," Officer Elton said to Nancy.

"In that case," replied Nancy, "it's my guess that the van went to the left." She pointed to a sign which read: *Garwin, 50 miles*. "Isn't Garwin a fairly large city?" she queried.

"Yes."

"Perhaps the thieves headed that way to dispose of the stolen furniture."

The officer nodded approvingly. "Sounds reasonable," he said. "Well, in any case, we can't go much farther, because we're near the state line."

Nancy had another thought. "I'll take the road to Garwin and swing around toward River Heights." She smiled. "If I see those thieves, I'll let you know."

"Well, you watch out, young lady. Those men may lock you up again!"

"I will. Anyhow, there'll be plenty of traffic as soon as I reach the main highway."

Without giving the policemen an opportunity

for further objection, Nancy started up and swung her car to the left. She noted in her rear-view mirror that the squad car had turned onto the right-hand road.

"The officers must have picked up a clue," Nancy said to herself. "But I certainly wish I could spot that van and maybe find a chance to look in the old clock!"

Nancy soon reached the main road. As mile after mile of highway spun behind her, Nancy's hopes grew dim. There were a number of side roads, any one of which the moving van might have taken to elude pursuers.

The young sleuth decided to adhere to her original theory—that Sid and his pals had headed for Garwin—and kept on the main highway.

"Those thieves think Jeff and I are still locked up and won't suspect they're being followed," she assured herself. Smiling, she thought hopefully, "In that case they won't be on their guard!"

About ten minutes later Nancy stopped at a service station to have her car refueled, and on impulse asked the attendant, "Did you by any chance see a moving van pass here recently?"

"Sure did, miss," was the prompt answer. "About half an hour ago. I noticed it because the driver was going at a terrific speed for a van."

Heartened, Nancy thanked him and resumed her pursuit, going past the turn for River Heights. "If only I can overtake the truck and somehow examine the Crowley clock before I have to report to the police!" she thought.

Again time elapsed and Nancy still saw no sign of a moving van on the highway. It was growing dusk and she decided that she would have to admit defeat.

"I never caught up to them." She sighed in disappointment, and turning into the opposite lane, headed back for the River Heights road.

Just then Nancy recalled that a little beyond the service station where she had stopped, she had noticed a rather run-down old inn. It was a slim hope, she knew, but the thieves might have put their van behind it while having a meal there.

"I'll go in and ask, anyhow," she decided.

Nancy increased her speed as much as she dared and within a few minutes came in sight of the inn. It stood back from the road a short distance and was half-hidden by tall trees. In front of the building a battered sign bearing the name *Black Horse Inn* creaked back and forth from a post. There was no sign of the van. Beyond the inn Nancy glimpsed a garage and a large barn. The doors to both were closed.

"I wonder," mused Nancy, "if the moving van is parked inside either one."

At the far side of the inn was a small woods with a narrow road leading into it. For safety's sake, Nancy thought it best to park her car on this little-used road.

She turned off the car lights, pocketed the key, and walked back to the curving driveway leading to the inn. As Nancy made her way forward, her heart pounded. There were tire marks which could belong to Sid's van! They led to the barn!

"Maybe those thieves are eating," she thought. "I'll look."

As Nancy stepped onto the porch, the sound of raucous laughter reached her ears. She tiptoed to a window and peered inside. What the young sleuth saw made her gasp, but she felt a glow of satisfaction.

In a dingy, dimly lighted room three men were seated about a table, eating voraciously. They were the thieves who had robbed the Topham bungalow!

CHAPTER XV

Nancy's Risky Undertaking

"I MUST notify the police at once!" Nancy told herself as she recognized the three thieves.

Turning away from the window, she crept noiselessly from the porch. She was about to make a dash for her car when a sudden thought occurred to her.

"If the gang have parked their van in the barn, now's my chance to look for the Crowley clock. I'm sure those men will be eating for a while, or they may even be staying overnight."

Acting on the impulse, Nancy sprinted to her car. Hastily she snatched a flashlight from the compartment, since it was now dark outside.

She made her way cautiously to the rear of the inn. Reaching the barn, she tried the closed doors, her heart pounding. They had not been locked!

As she slid back one of the doors, it squeaked in an alarming fashion. Anxiously Nancy glanced toward the inn, but so far as she could tell, her actions were unobserved. There was no one in sight.

Focusing her flashlight, she peered hopefully into the dark interior. A cry of satisfaction escaped her lips.

In front of her stood the moving van!

"What luck!" she exclaimed, snapping off her light.

With a last cautious glance in the direction of the inn, she hastily stepped inside and closed the barn door. With it shut, the interior of the barn was pitch dark.

Nancy switched on her flashlight again and played it over the moving van. She saw that its rear doors were closed.

Securing a firm grip on the handle, she gave it a quick turn. To her dismay the door did not open. The thieves had locked the van!

"Oh dear! Now what shall I do?" she wondered frantically. "I'll never be able to break the lock."

Desperately Nancy glanced about. She dared not remain many minutes in the barn, lest the thieves return and find her there. But she had to find out whether the Crowley clock was in the van.

"Perhaps the keys were left in the ignition," Nancy thought hopefully.

She rushed to the front of the van and clambered into the driver's seat. But there were no keys hanging from the ignition lock.

Nancy's mind worked frantically. She must find the keys! Perhaps the men had not taken them into the inn but had concealed them in the truck. Suddenly she remembered that people sometimes hide automobile keys under the floor mat. It was barely possible that the thieves had done this.

Hastily she pulled up a corner of the mat. Her flashlight revealed a small ring of keys!

"Luck was with me this time," she murmured, and quickly snatching up the ring, she ran back to the rear of the van.

After trying several of the keys, she at last found one which fitted the lock. Turning it, she jerked open the door. Nancy flashed her light about inside the truck. To her joy she recognized the van's contents as the furniture stolen from the Topham cottage!

"What will I do if the clock is on the bottom of the load?" Nancy wondered as she surveyed the pile of furniture. "I'll never find it."

Dexterously she swung herself up into the truck and flashed the light slowly about on chairs, tables, rugs, and boxes. There was no sign of the Crowley clock.

Then the beam rested for a moment on an object in a far corner. With a low cry of delight, Nancy saw that her search had been rewarded. Protected by a blanket, an old-fashioned mantel clock rested on top of a table in the very front of the van!

The young sleuth scrambled over the pieces of furniture as she tried to reach the clock. Her dress caught on something sharp and tore. Finally she arrived within arm's reach of the blanket. She grasped it and carefully pulled the clock toward her.

One glance at the timepiece assured her that it fitted the description Abby Rowen had given her. It had a square face and the top was ornamented with a crescent.

"The Crowley clock at last!" Nancy whispered almost unbelievingly.

But as she stood staring at it, her keen ears detected the sound of voices. The thieves!

"I'll be caught!" flashed through her mind. "And I won't be able to escape a second time!"

Clutching the blanket and the clock tightly in her arms, Nancy scrambled over the piled-up furniture as she struggled to get out of the truck before it was too late.

Reaching the door, she leaped lightly to the floor. She could now hear heavy footsteps coming closer and closer.

Nancy shut the truck doors as quickly as possible, and searched wildly for the keys.

"Oh, what did I do with them?" she thought frantically.

She saw that they had fallen to the floor and snatched them up. Hurriedly inserting the correct key in the lock, she secured the doors.

But as Nancy wheeled about she heard men's angry voices directly outside. Already someone was starting to slide back the barn door!

"Oh, what shall I do?" Nancy thought in despair. "I'm cornered!"

She realized instantly that she could not hope to run to the front of the car and place the keys under the mat where she had found them. "I'll just put them on the floor," she decided quickly. "Maybe the men will think they dropped them."

Then, glancing frantically about for a hiding place, Nancy saw an empty grain bin. Running to it, still holding the clock, she climbed inside and dropped the blanket over her head just as one of the barn doors slid open.

One of the men was speaking loudly. Nancy recognized the voice instantly. It belonged to Sid, the ringleader of the thieves.

"You had enough to eat," he growled. "We're goin' to get out of here before we have the cops down on our heads."

He climbed into the cab and turned on the headlights. Nancy held her breath. Would her hiding place be discovered? But the men apparently did not even look toward the bin.

In a moment Sid cried out, "What did you do with those keys? Thought you put 'em under the floor mat."

"I did."

"Well, they ain't here."

"Honest, boss, I—"

"Then come and find 'em, and don't be all night about it either!"

"All right. Get out of the way and give me a chance!"

As Jake went to the truck and began a careful search for the keys, Nancy listened fearfully from her hiding place.

"Say, if you've lost 'em—" the leader did not finish the threat, for at that moment the third man announced:

"Here they are on the floor! You must have thought you'd put 'em in your pocket, Jake, and dropped 'em instead."

"I didn't!" the other retorted.

The thieves were obviously in a quarrelsome mood. Just then the leader interposed:

"Cut out the yaking! We ain't got no time for a fight unless we want to land behind bars!"

"And if we do, it'll be your fault, Sid Sax. You left that girl to starve—"

"Shut up!" the leader snarled.

After a few more angry words, the three thieves climbed into the front seat and in a moment the engine started.

In relief Nancy heard the men go. The moment they were a safe distance from the barn, she climbed out of the bin.

Nancy watched long enough to make certain that the van had taken the road to Garwin. Then, snatching up her flashlight and clutching the precious clock in her arms, she turned and ran. "I'd better cut through the woods," she decided.

As Nancy darted among the trees, she cast an anxious glance over her shoulder, but to her intense relief she saw that she was not being followed. There seemed to be no one in the vicinity of the Black Horse Inn.

"I had a narrow escape that time," the young sleuth told herself as she ran. "I hate to think what might have happened if I had been discovered!" She clutched the mantel clock more tightly in her arms. "But it was worth the risk I took! I found the clock and maybe the secret of Josiah Crowley's will!"

Reaching the car, Nancy sprang inside. She took the key from her pocket and inserted it in the ignition lock.

"I'll notify the police as fast as I can," she decided. "Perhaps the state troopers can catch those men before they dispose of the furniture."

Then, just as Nancy was about to start the motor, her glance fell upon the Crowley clock which she had placed on the seat beside her. Did it contain old Josiah's mysterious notebook as she suspected?

"Oh, I must find out!" She got her flashlight.

Since the clock was too unwieldy to open inside the car, Nancy stepped out and laid it on the ground. She unfastened the glass door and ran her

hand around the walls. There was nothing inside. She tried the back. Only the mechanism of
the timepiece was there.

"Gone!" Nancy groaned. "Oh dear! Has my
luck run out?"

Could it be, she wondered, that the Tophams
had discovered the notebook only to destroy it?
Nancy discarded this thought as quickly as it came
to mind, for she recalled the conversation she had
overheard between Ada and Isabel. No, the Tophams were as ignorant as herself concerning the
location of a later will.

It was more likely that Abby Rowen had been
confused in her story. After all, she had not declared that the notebook would be found inside
the clock. Nancy herself had made the deduction.

"I was almost certain I'd find the notebook," she
murmured in disappointment. But a moment
later she took heart again. "It *must* be here somewhere," she told herself.

Turning the clock upside down, Nancy gave it a
hard shake. Something inside moved. Hopefully she repeated the action.

"Unless I'm wrong," Nancy thought excitedly,
"there's something inside this clock besides the
works!" She examined it more closely. "An extra piece of cardboard back of the face! And something in between the two! The notebook maybe!"

After a vain attempt to remove the heavy cardboard face with her fingers, Nancy took a small

screw driver from the glove compartment. With the tool it required but an instant to remove the two hands of the clock and jerk off the face.

As the cardboard fell to the floor, Nancy peered inside and gave a low cry of joy.

There, at one side of the clock, attached to a hook in the top, dangled a tiny dark-blue notebook!

CHAPTER XVI

The Capture

EAGERLY Nancy removed the little notebook from the hook. By holding the book directly under the beam of her flashlight, she could make out the words on the cover:

Property of Josiah Crowley.

"I've found it at last!" she thought excitedly.

Quickly turning the first few pages, she saw that they were yellowed with age. The writing was fine and cramped, and the ink had faded. The pages were crowded with business notations, and it was difficult to make out the words.

Nancy was thrilled, for she was positive that the notebook would disclose what Josiah Crowley had done with his last will. Yet, she realized that she could not hope to read through the book without a considerable loss of precious time. She must not delay another instant in reporting to the police.

"I'll read the notebook later," she decided, and

tucked it into her pocket. Then she put the clock together.

Hurriedly laying the timepiece back on the car seat, Nancy covered it with her coat and slid behind the wheel. Starting the engine, she swung the convertible onto the highway. Nancy cast an anxious glance in the direction the thieves had taken, and watched for side roads down which the men might turn to avoid the main highway.

"Perhaps I'd better phone the State Police from the first service station or store I come to."

Then suddenly she noticed a sign: *Alternate route to Garwin. Main road under repair.*

Reaching the intersection, she stopped to see if the familiar tire marks of the van indicated it had turned onto this dirt road. It had!

"Now what shall I do?"

As Nancy debated, she saw a car coming toward her. Her hopes soared. She could not be mistaken—it was a police prowl car with a red revolving roof light!

Instantly Nancy grabbed her own flashlight and jumped from the car. Standing at the side of the road, she waved her light and in a few minutes the police sedan stopped.

"I'm Nancy Drew," she said hurriedly to the two men inside. "Are you looking for the furniture thieves in the van?"

"Yes, we are. You're the girl who reported them?"

Nancy nodded, then pointed down the side road. "I think those are their tire marks. The men were at the Black Horse Inn, but left."

"You can identify them?" the driver asked.

"Oh, yes."

"Then please follow us. I'll radio for a car to approach the thieves' van from the other end of the road."

The police car sped down the bad road to Garwin, with Nancy following closely behind. They rode for several miles.

"Oh dear," thought Nancy, "I must have been wrong! We should have overtaken the van by this time."

Another ten minutes passed. Then, unexpectedly, she caught a glimpse of a red taillight on the road far ahead.

"It must be the van!" Nancy told herself hopefully. "The light doesn't appear to be moving fast enough for an automobile."

Evidently the police were of the same opinion, for at that moment their car slowed down. Nancy figured they would not stop the van until they saw the other police car arriving from the opposite direction. A few moments later she could see headlights in the distance.

The squad car in front of Nancy now sped ahead and pulled up alongside the van. "Pull over!" one of the officers shouted to the man in the cab.

Instead of doing so, the van put on a burst of

speed. But in order to avoid smashing into the oncoming squad car, the driver pulled too far to the right. The van swerved sharply. Its two right wheels went off into a deep ditch, and the vehicle toppled over.

In an instant the officers were out of the car and had the fugitives covered.

By this time Nancy, who had stopped her car at the side of the road, came running up. One of the officers turned to her and asked, "Can you identify these men?"

As a light was flashed upon each of the thieves in turn, Nancy nodded. "This one is Sid, who locked me in the closet," she declared, pointing to the leader. "The others are Jake and Parky."

The prisoners stared in complete disbelief. They were astounded to see Nancy Drew standing there. When it dawned on Sid that she evidently was responsible for their capture, he started to say something, then changed his mind and remained silent. The prisoners were quickly identified from licenses and other papers as wanted criminals.

One of the other officers opened the rear of the van and asked Nancy if she could identify the stolen furniture.

"Some of it," she replied. "That desk was taken from the room in which I was locked in the closet."

"Good enough," said the trooper. "These men will get long sentences for this. They'll be held

on several charges.   Are you willing to go with us
and prefer charges against them?"

"Yes, if it's necessary," Nancy promised reluctantly.   "But I don't live in this county and I'm
eager to get home right away.   Don't you have
enough evidence against them?   I think they're
the same men who stole several silver heirlooms
from the Turner sisters."

Sid and his companions winced, but did not
speak.

"I see," said the trooper. "Well, I guess there's
no need for you to go to headquarters now," the
officer admitted.   "I'll take your address, and if
your testimony should be required, I'll get in
touch with you."

When Nancy showed her driver's license as iden-
tification, the policeman glanced at her with new
interest.   Taking her aside, he said, "So you're the
daughter of Carson Drew!   I see you're following
in his footsteps.   Starting rather young, aren't
you?"

Nancy laughed. "It was only by accident that I
arrived at the Topham bungalow at the critical
moment," she protested modestly.

"Not many girls would have used their wits the
way you did," the officer observed.   "Unless I'm
mistaken, these fellows are old hands at this game.
They're no doubt the men who have been stealing
various things from around Moon Lake for a number of seasons.   The residents will be mighty

grateful for what you've done. And that Mrs. Topham you spoke of—she ought to give you a liberal reward for saving her household goods."

Nancy shook her head. "I don't want a reward, really I don't."

"Just the same you've earned one," insisted the officer, who said his name was Cowen. "If you'd like, I'll tell my chief the whole story and he'll take the matter up with this Mrs. Topham."

"You don't know her," Nancy remarked, "and I do. She'd never offer a reward. Even if she did, I wouldn't accept it." After a slight pause, she added, "In fact, I prefer that my name not be mentioned to her at all."

Officer Cowen shook his head in disbelief. "Well, all right, then. If you're sure you don't want any credit for capturing the thieves, I won't say anything. You're certain?"

"I am," Nancy replied firmly, "for a particular reason of my own."

The trooper smiled. "It must be a mighty good one."

"There *is* one favor you might do me," said Nancy. "Ask your chief to put in a good word for the caretaker, Jeff Tucker, to the Tophams. Perhaps then he won't lose his job."

"Be glad to," Officer Cowen promised. "And if you're really anxious not to figure in the case, I'll see if we can get along without your testimony."

Nancy thanked him, then suddenly thought of

the old clock. At the moment it was lying on the front seat of her car, less than a dozen yards away. Should she reveal this information? She decided against doing so in front of the thieves, who, though they could not hear what she had been saying, could see everything plainly. "I'll wait until a more opportune time," Nancy concluded.

It was agreed among the state policemen that one of them would stay to guard the van and keep a radio car standing by there. The other three troopers would take the captive thieves to headquarters.

The three prisoners, their faces sullen, were crowded into the car. One of the troopers took the wheel, while the one beside him kept the handcuffed trio closely covered.

Officer Cowen, a strapping, husky man, turned to Nancy. "I'll ride with you," he said. "You're going past headquarters on the main road?"

"I'm on my way to River Heights," she responded.

"Then the station is on your route. You can drop me off if you will."

"Why—why, of course," Nancy stammered. "I'll be glad to."

At once she had thought of the Crowley clock. What if Officer Cowen should not accept her explanation as to why she had helped herself to the heirloom and its strange contents? If this happened, her progress in solving the mystery might

receive a serious setback! Even as these disturb-
ing ideas raced through her mind, the trooper
started toward the blue convertible.

Nancy braced herself. "I'll just have to 'fess
up," she said to herself, "and take the conse-
quences!"

CHAPTER XVII

Strange Instructions

FOR THE next few seconds Nancy's mind worked
like lightning as she rehearsed what she would
say to Officer Cowen.   One idea stood out clearly:
the police were concerned in the theft of the furniture, so she would hand over the clock.   But they
were not involved in locating Mr. Crowley's missing will.   For this reason the young sleuth felt jus-
tified in keeping the notebook.   She would turn
it over to her father, and let him decide what dis-
position should be made of it.

"After all," Nancy told herself, "Dad is handling
the Crowley case for the Hoovers, and even the
Turners and Mrs. Rowen, in a way."

By this time she and the trooper had reached
her car.   "Would you like me to drive?" he asked.

"Why—er—yes, if you wish," Nancy replied.
"But first I want to show you something," she

added, as he opened the door for her. "I have some stolen property here."

"What!"

Quickly Nancy explained that she had taken the responsibility of trying to learn whether or not the van held the stolen furniture. "I recognized a few of the pieces, and possibly this clock which the Tophams had told me about. I took that out to examine it. Then I never had a chance to get it back without being caught. I'm sure the Tophams will identify the old clock as their property."

Nancy's explanation seemed to satisfy the officer. "I'll take it to headquarters," he said. "Let's go!"

He laid the clock on the rear seat, then slid behind the wheel and drove off.

It was nearly midnight when Nancy, tired and worn from her long ride, reached the Drew home in River Heights. As she drove into the double garage, she noticed that her father's car was gone. A glance at the house disclosed that the windows were dark, with the exception of a light in the hall. Hannah Gruen must be in bed.

"Of course she's not expecting me," Nancy reasoned. "I wonder where Dad can be? Oh, I hope he'll get home soon. I want to tell him about my discovery right away."

After locking the garage door, she went to the kitchen entrance and let herself in.

Her eyes lighted on the refrigerator and suddenly Nancy realized she was very hungry. Many hours had passed since she had eaten. "Um, food!" she thought.

Just as Nancy opened the refrigerator door, she heard steps on the stairs and Hannah Gruen, wearing a sleepy look, appeared in robe and slippers.

"Nancy!" cried the housekeeper, instantly wide awake.

"Surprise, Hannah darling!" Nancy gave the housekeeper an affectionate hug and kiss. "I'm simply starved. Haven't had a bite since lunchtime."

"Why, you poor dear!" the housekeeper exclaimed in concern. "What happened? I'll fix you something right away."

As the two prepared a chicken sandwich, some cocoa, and Hannah cut a large slice of cinnamon cake over which she poured hot applesauce, Nancy told of her adventures.

The housekeeper's eyes widened. "Nancy, you might have been killed by those awful men. Well, I'm certainly glad they've been captured."

"So am I!" declared Nancy fervently as she finished the last crumb of cake. "And I hope the Turners get back their silver heirlooms."

"How about the Tophams?" Hannah Gruen questioned teasingly.

"Somehow," said Nancy with a wink, "that doesn't seem to worry me." Then she asked, "Where's Dad?"

"Working at his office," Hannah Gruen replied. "He phoned earlier that something unexpected had come up in connection with one of his cases."

"Then I'll wait for him," said Nancy. "You go back to bed. And thanks a million." The sleepy housekeeper did not demur.

Left alone, Nancy tidied the kitchen, then went to the living room.

"Now to find out what became of Josiah Crowley's last will," she thought excitedly, as she curled up in a comfortable chair near a reading lamp.

Carefully she thumbed the yellowed pages, for she was afraid they might tear. Evidently Josiah Crowley had used the same notebook for many years.

"He certainly knew how to save money," she mused.

Nancy read page after page, perusing various kinds of memoranda and many notations of property owned by Mr. Crowley. There were also figures on numerous business transactions in which he had been involved. Nancy was surprised at the long list of stocks, bonds, and notes which apparently belonged to the estate.

"I had no idea Josiah Crowley was worth so much," she murmured.

After a time Nancy grew impatient at the seemingly endless list of figures. She skipped several pages of the little notebook, and turned toward the end where Mr. Crowley had listed his possessions.

"Why, what's this?" she asked herself. Fastened to one page was a very thin, flat key with a tag marked 148.

Suddenly a phrase on the opposite page, "My last will and testament," caught and held Nancy's attention. Eagerly she began to read the whole section.

"I've found it!" she exclaimed excitedly. "I'm glad I didn't give up the search!"

The notation concerning the will was brief. Nancy assumed the cramped writing was Josiah Crowley's. It read:

To whom it may concern: My last will and testament will be found in safe-deposit box number 148 in the Merchants Trust Company. The box is under the name of Josiah Johnston.

"And this is the key to the box!" Nancy told herself.

For several moments the young sleuth sat staring ahead of her. It seemed unbelievable that she had solved the mystery. But surely there could no mistake. The date of the entry in the notebook was recent and the ink had not faded as it had on the earlier pages.

"There *is* a later will!" Nancy exclaimed aloud. "Oh, if only it leaves something to the Turners, and the Mathews, and Abby Rowen, and the Hoover girls! Then Allison could take voice lessons and little Judy would be taken care of, and—"

Nancy hurriedly read on, hoping to learn something definite. But although she carefully examined every page in the book, there was no other mention of the will, nor any clue to its contents.

"No wonder the document didn't come to light," Nancy mused. "Who would have thought of looking for it in a safe-deposit box under the name of Josiah Johnston? In his desire for safe-keeping, Josiah Crowley nearly defeated his own purpose."

Her thoughts were interrupted as she heard a car turn into the driveway. Rushing to the window, Nancy saw her father pull into the garage. She ran to meet him at the kitchen door.

"Why, hello, Nancy," he greeted her in surprise. "If I had known you were here, I'd have come home sooner. I was doing some special work on a case. Back from Moon Lake ahead of schedule, aren't you?"

"Yes," Nancy admitted, trying to hide her excitement. "But for a good reason."

Before her father could hang up his hat in the hall closet, she plunged into the story of her adventures and ended by showing him the notebook which she had found inside the mantel clock. When she had finished, Carson Drew stared at his daughter with mingled pride and amazement.

"You're a good detective, Nancy. You've picked up an excellent clue," he said.

"Dad, I thought it best not tell the police about

the notebook. We don't want to reveal the secret of another will to the executor mentioned in the old one."

"You mean Mr. Topham. I agree," the lawyer replied. "The new will may name someone else as executor." He smiled. "I think you and I should try to see this will. But," he added, "which Merchants Trust Company is it in? There must be dozens of banks by that name."

Nancy suddenly snapped her fingers. "Dad, I believe I know. You recall that Judge Hart and his wife told me they had seen Josiah Crowley in Masonville a couple of times. And there's a Merchants Trust Company there."

Mr. Drew looked at his daughter admiringly. "I believe you have the answer, Nancy. And Judge Hart is just the man to help us. I'll phone him in the morning. Well, I guess we both need some sleep."

As the lawyer kissed his daughter good night, he added, "My dear, you were in serious danger when you encountered those thieves. I don't like to have you take such risks. I am very grateful indeed that you are back home safe."

"The Tophams aren't going to thank me when they find out what I have done," Nancy said, as she went up the stairs ahead of her father. "In fact, we may have a battle on our hands, Dad."

"That's right, Nancy. And it will be just as well that they don't learn the details of how the will was found until the matter is settled beyond a doubt."

"I'm certainly curious to find out if the new will left anything to the Tophams," said Nancy.

"If not," her father put in, "your discovery will strike them at an especially awkward time."

Nancy paused on the stairs and turned to face her father. "What do you mean?"

"Well, there's talk about town that Richard Topham has been losing heavily in the stock market this past month. He has been getting credit at a number of places on the strength of the inheritance, and I suspect he is depending on Crowley's money to pull him through a tight spot. He's making every effort to speed up the settlement of the estate."

"Then we'd better hurry," said Nancy, resuming the climb.

"Don't build your hopes too high," Mr. Drew advised her wisely. "There may be a slip, you know."

"How?"

"We may fail to find the will in the safe-deposit box."

"Oh, I can't believe it, Dad. The notebook says it's there!"

"Then," the lawyer continued, "there is a chance that Josiah Crowley didn't dispose of the fortune as the Turners and the Hoovers and others expected he would."

"But he promised all those people—"

"I know, Nancy. But there's just the possibility that the notation in the notebook was wishful thinking and Mr. Crowley never got around to making the new will."

"You can discourage me all you want to, Dad, but I'm not going to stop hoping!" Nancy said. "Oh, I can scarcely wait for morning to come!"

Her father laughed. "You're an incurable optimist! Now put Josiah Crowley out of your mind and get a good night's sleep."

At the door of her bedroom Nancy hesitated, then turned back toward the stairs.

"What's up?" Mr. Drew asked.

Without answering Nancy ran down to the living room, picked up the notebook which lay on the table, and hurried back up the carpeted steps.

"After all I've gone through to get my hands on this," she told her father, "I'm not going to take any chances!" Nancy laughed. "Tonight I'll sleep with it under my pillow!"

CHAPTER XVIII

A Suspenseful Search

WHEN Nancy awoke the following morning, bright sunlight was streaming through her open bedroom window. As her eyes turned toward the clock on her dresser, she was alarmed to see that it was a little after nine o'clock.

"How could I have overslept on a morning like this?" she chided herself.

Quickly running her hand under the pillow, she brought out the Crowley notebook and surveyed it with satisfaction.

"What a surprise the Tophams are going to get!" she murmured softly.

After hastily bathing and dressing, Nancy hurried downstairs looking very attractive in a blue summer sweater suit. She kissed Hannah Gruen, who said a cheery good morning and told Nancy that Mr. Drew had already left for his office.

"Oh dear," Nancy said, "I wonder if he forgot our date?"

"No indeed," the housekeeper replied. "He phoned Judge Hart and expects word from him by ten o'clock. He'll let you know the result. My goodness, Nancy, you've really made a big discovery. I do hope everything turns out for the best."

She went into the kitchen but returned in a moment with a plate of crisp, golden waffles.

"Better eat your breakfast," she advised. "Your dad may call any minute."

Nancy ate a dish of strawberries, then started on the waffles. "These are yummy," she stated, pouring maple syrup over a second one.

She had just finished eating when the phone rang. Mr. Drew was calling to say Judge Hart had made arrangements at the bank. "Come to my office with the notebook and key, Nancy. We'll start from here."

"I'll be right down, Dad."

Nancy went upstairs for her purse, then drove to her father's office.

"I have the notebook with me," she told the lawyer. "Do you want it?"

"We'll take the book along. I want to show it to the head of the trust department at the bank," Mr. Drew said. "It's our proof we have good reason for taking a look in Mr. Crowley's box."

After leaving a number of instructions with his private secretary, Carson Drew followed his daughter from the office. He took his place beside her in the convertible.

"I'll never get over it if we don't find a newer will," Nancy declared, as they drove along. A flush of excitement had tinted her cheeks and her eyes were bright.

"You must remember one thing, Nancy," returned her father calmly. "Crowley was an odd person and did things in an odd way. A will may be there, and again it may not. Perhaps he only left further directions to finding it.

"I remember one case in Canada years ago. An eccentric Frenchman died and left directions to look in a trunk of old clothes for a will. In the pocket of a coat were found further instructions to look in a closet of his home. There his family found a note telling them to look in a copper boiler.

"The boiler had disappeared but was finally located in a curiosity shop. Inside, pasted on the bottom, was what proved to be a word puzzle in Chinese. The old Frenchman's heirs were about to give up in despair when a Chinese solved the puzzle and the old man's fortune was found—a bag of gold under a board in his bedroom floor!"

"At least they found it," said Nancy.

The trip to Masonville was quickly accomplished, and Nancy parked the car in front of the Merchants Trust Company.

Father and daughter alighted and entered the

bank. Mr. Drew gave his name and asked to see the president. After a few minutes' wait they were ushered into a private conference room. An elderly man, Mr. Jensen, arose to greet them.

The introductions over, Mr. Drew hastened to state his mission. Before he could finish the story, the bank president broke in.

"Judge Hart has told me the story. I'll call Mr. Warren, our trust officer."

He picked up his desk phone and in a few minutes Mr. Warren appeared and was introduced. Nancy now brought out the notebook, opened it to the important page, and handed it to the men to read.

When they finished, Mr. Jensen said, "What a mystery!"

Mr. Warren pulled from his pocket the file card which the owner of Box 148 had filled out in the name of Josiah Johnston. The two samples of cramped handwritings were compared.

"I would say," Mr. Drew spoke up, "that there is no doubt but that Crowley and Johnston were the same person."

"I agree," asserted Mr. Jensen, and his trust officer nodded.

"Then there's no reason why we shouldn't open the box?" Mr. Drew asked.

"None," Mr. Warren replied. "Of course nothing may be removed, you understand."

"All I want to see," Nancy spoke up, "is whether

there is a will in the box, the date on it, who the executor is, and who the heirs are."

The bankers smiled and Mr. Jensen said, "You're hoping to solve four mysteries all at once! Well, let's get started."

With Mr. Warren in the lead, the four walked toward the rear of the bank to the vault of the trust department. A guard opened the door and they went through. Mr. Jensen took the key from Mr. Crowley's notebook, while Mr. Warren opened the first part of the double safety lock with the bank key. Then he inserted the key from the notebook. It fitted!

In a moment he lifted out Deposit Box Number 148. It was a small one and not heavy, he said.

"We'll take this into a private room," Mr. Jensen stated. He, Nancy, and Mr. Drew followed the trust officer down a corridor of cubbyhole rooms until they reached one not in use.

"Now," said Mr. Jensen, when the door was closed behind them, "we shall see how many—if any—of the mysteries are solved."

Nancy held her breath as he raised the lid of the box. All peered inside. The box was empty, except for one bulky document in the bottom.

"Oh, it must be the will!" Nancy exclaimed.

"It is a will," Mr. Jensen announced, after a hasty glance at the first page. "Josiah Crowley's last will and testament."

"When was it written?" Nancy asked quickly.

"In March of this year," Mr. Jensen told her.

"Oh, Dad," Nancy cried, "this was later than the will the Tophams submitted for probate!"

"That's right."

"Let's read it right away," Nancy begged.

Mr. Jensen handed the sheets to Mr. Drew. "Maybe you can decipher this. The handwriting is too much for me."

The lawyer took the will. Then, as Nancy looked over his shoulder, he haltingly read aloud, giving an interpretation rather than a word by word account.

"Mr. Jensen—Mr. Warren, your bank has been named as executor," he said.

"Very good." The president smiled. "But I expect Mr. Topham won't be happy to hear this."

Mr. Drew had turned to the last page. "The signature of Josiah is in order," he remarked, "and there are two witnesses—Dr. Nesbitt and Thomas Wackley. No wonder this will didn't come to light. Both those men died in April."

As Nancy tried to decipher the handwriting, she noticed to her delight that the Hoover girls and Abby Rowen were mentioned.

At this moment the president said, "Mr. Drew, the bank's regular lawyer had just left for Europe on an extended vacation. Since you and your daughter have solved the mystery and are so vitally interested in it, would you handle this case for us?"

*Nancy held her breath as Mr. Jensen opened the
safe-deposit box*

Nancy's eyes sparkled and Mr. Drew smiled. "I'd certainly be very glad to," he said.

"What instructions have you for us?" Mr. Warren asked.

Mr. Drew thought a moment, then said, "Because of the unusual aspects of this case, I believe that first of all I'd like you to have photostats of the will made, so I can study the contents carefully."

"We'll be happy to do that," Mr. Jensen replied. "And then?"

"After I'm sure everything is legal," Mr. Drew went on, "I'll deliver the original will for probate and notify the people who will benefit from Mr. Crowley's estate."

"Fine," said Mr. Jensen. "We have photostating equipment right here. I'll have a couple of copies made while you wait. Or shall I send them to your office?"

Mr. Drew glanced at his daughter. "We'll wait," he said, smiling.

While the photostats were being made, Nancy's mind was racing. "Oh, I hope Allison receives enough money to pay for singing lessons, and the other deserving people get nice amounts," she whispered to her father, who nodded.

The wait seemed interminable to Nancy, who could not sit still. She walked back and forth until finally her father remarked teasingly, "You're like a caged lion."

Nancy pretended to pout. "At least I'm not growling," she said, and Mr. Drew grinned.

Soon a messenger brought back the will, together with two photostats of the document.

"Thank you," said Mr. Jensen, who handed the photostatic copies to Mr. Drew.

"I'll work on this at once," the lawyer promised as he put the papers in his brief case. Then he and his daughter left the bank.

Mr. Drew insisted that he and Nancy stop for lunch and refused to let her look at the will while they were waiting to be served. "Relax, young lady," he warned. "There's no point in letting any prying eyes know our secret."

As he saw his daughter's animation fading, Mr. Drew said, "Suppose you come to my office with me and we'll work on the problem together. I'll have the will typed. In this way its full meaning can be understood more easily."

"Oh, thanks, Dad," said Nancy.

In the lawyer's office the young sleuth sat down beside his typist, Miss Lamby. As each page came from the machine, Nancy read it avidly.

"Mr. Crowley certainly seemed to know the correct phraseology for drawing up a will," she remarked.

Finally, when the typing had been completed, Nancy said to the secretary, "I have a lot of questions to ask Dad."

Miss Lamby smiled. "If they're legal ones, he'll

know all the answers," she said. "There's no bet-ter lawyer in River Heights than your father."

Nancy smiled as she dashed into her father's of-fice. The two Drews sat down to study Josiah Crowley's last will and testament.

"If this does prove to be legal," said Nancy, "it will certainly be a blow to the Tophams."

"I'm afraid so."

"Dad, when you call a meeting of all the rela-tives and read the will aloud," Nancy said, "please may I be there?"

Mr. Drew laughed. "I'll humor you this time, Nancy. You may be present when the Tophams get the surprise of their lives!"

CHAPTER XIX

Startling Revelations

"Dad, it's nearly two o'clock now. Mr. Crowley's relatives should be here in a few minutes! I'm so excited!"

Carson Drew, who stood in the living room of the Drew home with Mr. Warren from the bank, smiled at his daughter as she fluttered about, arranging chairs.

"I believe you're more thrilled than if you were inheriting the fortune yourself," he remarked.

"I am thrilled," Nancy admitted. "I can scarcely wait until the will is read aloud. Won't everyone be surprised? Especially the Tophams. Do you think they will come?"

"Oh, yes, the Tophams will be here. And, unless I am mistaken, they will bring a lawyer with them. Just as soon as they learned that another will had come to light, they began to worry. They will certainly want to hear what is in this one."

"Are you certain the will we found can't be broken?" Nancy inquired anxiously.

"Of course I can't be certain, Nancy. But I have gone over it carefully, and so far as I can tell, it is technically perfect. I also asked a couple of lawyer friends and they agree. Josiah Crowley was peculiar in some ways, but he was a very smart man. I'll promise you the Tophams will have a difficult time if they try to contest this will."

"The bank will help you fight," Mr. Warren put in.

With the exception of Abby Rowen, who was still confined to bed, all the old gentleman's relatives had promised to be present. Grace and Allison Hoover, although not relatives, had also been invited.

"It's too bad Mrs. Rowen can't come," said Nancy. "But I'll take the news to her this very afternoon."

"The size of the fortune will probably be a great surprise to everyone but the Tophams," said her father with a smile. "Nancy, you did a remarkable piece of detective work."

"It was fun," she said modestly. "And I can hardly wait to have it all cleared up."

"We may have some trying minutes with the Tophams, Nancy," her father warned.

"Yes, I suppose so. I expect anybody would be sorry to see a fortune slip away. . . . Dad, I see

Grace and Allison coming up the walk now," Nancy announced, glancing out the window.

She greeted them with kisses and escorted the sisters into the living room, where she introduced them to Mr. Warren. As Allison sat down, she whispered to Nancy:

"Is it true a later will has been found?"

"You and Grace have no cause to worry," Nancy assured her with a mysterious smile.

The doorbell rang. This time Nancy admitted Edna and Mary Turner, who were dressed as if for a party. With them was little Judy, who threw herself into Nancy's arms. A few minutes later the Mathews brothers, William and Fred, arrived.

"I guess everyone is here except the Tophams," Mr. Drew commented. "We had better wait for them a few minutes."

There was no need to wait, for at that moment the bell rang sharply. Nancy opened the door and the four members of the Topham family walked in haughtily, merely nodding to the others in the room. As Mr. Drew had predicted, they were accompanied by a lawyer.

"Why have we been called here?" Mrs. Topham demanded, addressing Mr. Drew. "Have you the audacity to claim that another will has been found?"

"I have a will written only this past March, Mrs. Topham," Carson Drew replied evenly. "And I'd like to introduce to all of you Mr. John Warren, trust officer of the Merchants Trust Company, of Masonville, which has been named as executor."

"It's preposterous!" Mrs. Topham stormed. "Josiah Crowley made only one will and in that he left everything to us with my husband as executor."

"It looks like a conspiracy to me," Ada added tartly, as she gazed coldly upon the relatives and friends who were seated about the room.

Isabel did not speak, but tossed her head contemptuously. Richard Topham likewise did not offer a comment, but uneasily seated himself beside his own attorney.

"If you will please be seated, Mrs. Topham, I will read the will," Mr. Drew suggested.

Reluctantly Mrs. Topham sat down.

"As I have said," Mr. Drew began, "a recent will of the late Josiah Crowley was found in a safe-deposit box in the Masonville bank. The will is unusually long, and with your permission I will read from a typed copy only the portions which have to do with the disposal of the property. But first I want to ask Mr. Topham what value he puts on the estate."

"A hundred thousand after taxes," the man replied.

"Oh!" the Turners exclaimed, and Mary said, "I had no idea Josiah had that much money."

"Nor I," Edna agreed.

Mr. Drew picked up several typewritten sheets from the table, and began to read in a clear voice:

"'I, Josiah Crowley, do make this my last will and testament, hereby revoking all former wills by me at any time made. I give and bequeath all my property, real and personal, as follows:

"'To my beloved friends and neighbors, Grace and Allison Hoover, a sum equal to twenty per cent of my estate, share and share alike.'"

"I must be dreaming!" Grace gasped.

"You mean I'm going to get ten thousand dollars?" Allison cried out. She burst into tears. "Oh, Nancy, you did this for me! Now I can have my voice lessons."

Isabel Topham eyed her disdainfully. "It would take more than ten thousand dollars to make a singer out of you!" she said maliciously.

"Quiet!" commanded her father. "Let's hear what else this will says."

His daughter subsided, but his wife exclaimed spitefully, "The will is a fraud. The Hoovers aren't even relatives."

"It is no fraud," Mr. Drew told her quietly. Again he picked up the will and began to read:

"'To Abby Rowen, my late wife's cousin, in consideration of her kindness to me, a sum equal to ten per cent of my estate.'"

"Oh, I'm so glad," Grace murmured. "Now she'll be able to get the medical and other attention she needs."

"And have someone live at her house to take care of her," said Nancy.

"That old lady gets ten thousand dollars?" Ada Topham said harshly. "What did she ever do for Cousin Josiah?" Angrily she turned to her mother. "We took care of him for years—she didn't!"

"I'll say not," Isabel echoed, her voice tart.

" 'To my cousins, Fred and William Mathews, a sum equal to twenty per cent of my estate, share and share alike,' " Mr. Drew read.

"We didn't expect that much," Fred Mathews declared in genuine surprise. "Josiah was very kind." Fred smiled. "Now we can take a trip like we've always wanted to do, William."

"That's right. I just can't believe it. A long trip on an ocean liner or a plane."

" 'To my cousins, Edna and Mary Turner, twenty per cent of my estate, share and share alike.' "

"Oh, how generous!" Edna murmured. "Now little Judy can have the things we've always wanted to give her."

"Yes," said Mary Turner. "Oh, I feel so relieved."

"Aren't we mentioned at all?" Mrs. Topham broke in sharply.

Mr. Drew smiled. "Yes, you are mentioned. I'm coming to that now. 'To Richard Topham, five thousand dollars.   To Grace and Allison Hoover—' "

"Hold on!" cried Mrs. Topham.   "What about me and the girls?"

"No money was left to you," the lawyer stated simply.

Isabel gave a shriek.   "Oh, no!   Oh, no!   Oh, Mother, all those bills!   What'll we do?"

Ada too had cried out.   "I'll have to go to work! Oh, I can't bear the thought of it!"

When the furor died down, Mr. Drew read on, " 'To Grace and Allison Hoover my household furniture now in the possession of Mrs. Richard Topham.' "

There was a gasp of surprise from everyone in the room, and Mrs. Topham half arose from her chair.   It was generally known in River Heights that she had practically confiscated Josiah Crowley's furniture at the time he had been induced to make his home with the Tophams.

"How insulting!" the woman cried.   "Does Josiah Crowley dare hint that I took his furniture?"

"I'm sure I don't know what was in his mind at the time he wrote the will," Mr. Drew told her with a smile.

Grace Hoover interposed quickly, "We have enough furniture without Josiah Crowley's."

Allison nodded.   "We'll not take any of it from you, Mrs. Topham."

Mr. Drew carefully folded the document he had been reading, and after placing it in his pocket, he said to the people in the room:

"That is all, except that there is a proviso for the executor to pay all Mr. Crowley's just debts, including his funeral expenses, and that what balance is left in the estate goes to the Manningham Old Men's Home. I understand Josiah Crowley kept his assets in a liquid state. It will not be difficult to convert the estate into cash. For that reason I should think it would be possible to draw on your inheritances at once."

Ada wheeled upon Nancy, her face convulsed with anger. "You engineered this whole thing, Nancy Drew!" she accused bitterly.

"Any good I've done I'm happy about," Nancy answered.

"We'll break the will!" Mrs. Topham announced firmly.

CHAPTER XX

A Happy Finale

"OF COURSE you may take the matter into court if you like," Mr. Drew responded to Mrs. Topham's threat. "But I warn you it will be a waste of your time and money. If you don't wish to accept my judgment, ask your own lawyer."

"Mr. Drew is right," the other lawyer said, after arising and looking carefully at the legal document which Mr. Drew took from his pocket.

"Oh, he is, is he?" Mrs. Topham retorted. "If that's all you know about law, you're discharged! We'll get another lawyer and we'll fight to the last ditch!"

With that she arose and stalked from the room. Isabel and Ada followed, after bestowing a withering glance upon Nancy. Mr. Topham brought up the rear. As soon as the door had closed behind them, their lawyer arose and picked up his brief case.

"Well, I can't say I'm sorry to be taken off the case," he remarked as he, too, took his leave. "But I advise you to be on your guard. That woman is certainly belligerent."

At once the atmosphere in the Drew living room became less strained, though each person was fearful Mrs. Topham would make trouble. Everyone began to talk at once.

"Oh, Nancy, I can hardly believe it yet!" Allison declared happily. "The money means so much to Grace and me! And we owe it all to you, Nancy Drew! You haven't told us how you came to find the will, but I know you were responsible."

When the Hoover girls and Mr. Crowley's relatives begged her for the details, Nancy told of her adventure with the thieves at Moon Lake. After she had finished the story, they praised her highly for what she had done.

"We'll never be able to thank you enough," Grace said quietly. "But after the estate has been settled, we'll try to show our appreciation."

It was on the tip of Nancy's tongue to say that she did not want a reward, when Mr. Drew turned the conversation into a different channel.

"Mrs. Topham will not give up the money without a fight," he warned. "My advice would be to go along as you have until the court has decided to accept this will as the final one. However, if Mrs. Topham and her daughters bring the matter into court, I'll give them a battle they'll never forget!"

After thanking Mr. Drew and Nancy for everything they had done, the relatives and friends departed. Allison and Grace were the last to leave. On the porch, Allison paused to hug Nancy and say, "Please let us know what develops. I'm so eager to start taking voice lessons."

Nancy wanted to set off at once to see Abby Rowen and tell her the good news. But upon second thought she decided to wait. Suppose the Tophams succeeded in upsetting the whole case!

For a week Nancy waited impatiently to hear the result of the battle over the will. As she and her father had anticipated, Mrs. Topham was fighting bitterly for the Crowley estate. She had put forth the claim that the will Nancy had unearthed was a forged document.

"This suspense is just awful," Nancy told her father one morning. "When are we going to get final word?"

"I can't answer that, Nancy. But apparently Mr. Topham thinks it's a losing battle. I suppose you've heard about the family."

"Why, no, what about them?"

"They're practically bankrupt. Richard Topham has been losing steadily on the stock market of late. After his failure to recover the Crowley fortune, the banks reduced his credit. He's been forced to give up his beautiful home."

"No, really? How that must hurt Mrs. Topham and the two girls!"

"Yes, it's undoubtedly a bitter pill to swallow. They are moving into a small house this week, and from now on they'll have to give up their extravagant way of living. Both girls are working. Personally, I think it will be good for them."

Word came that the three furniture thieves had finally confessed to many robberies and their unsold loot was recovered. Among the pieces were all the heirlooms they had stolen from the Turners.

One evening Mr. Drew came home wearing a broad smile. Facing Nancy and laying both hands on her shoulders, he said:

"We've won, my dear. The will you located has been accepted as the last one Mr. Crowley wrote."

"Oh, Dad, how wonderful!" she cried, whirling her father about in a little dance. "First thing tomorrow morning, may I go and tell Allison and Grace and the others?"

"I think that would be a fine idea. Of course the bank and I will formally notify them later."

The following morning Nancy was the first one downstairs and started breakfast before Hannah Gruen appeared.

"My goodness, you're an early bird, Nancy," the housekeeper said with a smile. "Big day, eh?"

"*Very* big," Nancy replied.

As soon as the family had eaten, Hannah said,

"Never mind helping me today. You run along and make those people happy as soon as possible."

"Oh, thank you, Hannah. I'll leave right away."

Nancy, dressed in a simple green linen sports dress with a matching sweater, kissed her little family good-by and drove off. Her first stop was at the Mathews brothers. They greeted her affably, then waited for Nancy to speak.

"I have good news," she said, her eyes dancing. "Mrs. Topham lost her case. The will Dad and I found has been accepted for probate. You will receive the inheritance Mr. Crowley left you!"

"Praise be!" Fred cried. "And we never would have received it if it hadn't been for you." His brother nodded in agreement.

To cover her embarrassment at their praise, Nancy reached into a pocket and pulled out a handful of travel folders and airline schedules. "I thought you might like to look at these. Now I must hurry off and tell the other heirs."

As she drove away, the two men smiled, waved, then immediately began to look at the folders. "I hope they have a grand trip," Nancy thought.

Half an hour later she pulled into the driveway of the Turner home. Before the car stopped, Judy came racing from the front door. As Nancy stepped out, the little girl threw herself into the young sleuth's arms. "Nancy, guess what! My

aunties found an old, old doll that belonged to
my mommy and they gave it to me. Come and see
her. She's pretty as can be."

Judy pulled Nancy by the hand up the steps and
into the house. "There she is," the child said
proudly, pointing to a blond, curly-haired doll
seated in a tiny rocking chair.

"Why, she's darling," Nancy commented.
"And, Judy, she looks like you, dimples and all."

Judy nodded. "And Aunt Mary says she looks
like my mommy did when she was a little girl, so
I'm always going to take very good care of my
dolly."

At this moment her great-aunts came from the
rear of the house to greet their caller.

"I see," said Nancy, "that you have made Judy
very happy. Now it's my turn to pass along good
news to you," and she told about their inheritance.

The women smiled happily and tears came
to their eyes. Then suddenly Edna Turner gave
Nancy an impulsive hug. "You dear, dear girl!"
she half sobbed with joy. "Now Judy will always
be well taken care of and receive the kind of
schooling we think she should have!"

Mary kissed Nancy and thanked the young
sleuth for her untiring efforts to see justice done.
Judy, meanwhile, looked on in puzzlement at the
scene. But sensing that it called for her participa-
tion, she grabbed up her new doll and began to
dance around with it.

"Now you can go to school too, Carol," she told her doll.

It was hard for Nancy to break away from the Turners, but she reminded them that she still had two calls to make.

"But come back soon," Judy said.

When Nancy arrived at Abby Rowen's she was delighted to find her seated by the window in a chair. Her kind neighbor, Mrs. Jones, was there preparing food for the invalid. To this Nancy added a jar of homemade beef broth and a casserole of rice and chicken which Hannah Gruen had insisted upon sending.

"Can you stay a little while?" Mrs. Jones asked. "I ought to run home for half an hour, then I'll come back."

"She's been so kind," Abby Rowen spoke up. "Today she took my laundry home to wash and iron." After the woman had left, Abby went on, "The folks around here have been very thoughtful of me, but I just can't impose on them any longer. Yet I haven't any money—"

Nancy took the invalid's hand in hers and smiled. "I came to tell you that now you have lots of money, left to you by Josiah Crowley."

"What! You mean I won't have to depend on just my little pension any longer? Bless Josiah! Nancy, I never could believe that my cousin would go back on his word."

Nancy ate some broth and crackers with Abby

Rowen and told the whole story. The old woman's eyes began to sparkle and color came into her cheeks. "Oh, this is so wonderful!" she said. Then she chuckled. "It does my heart good to know you outwitted those uppity Topham women!"

Nancy grinned, then said soberly, "If I hadn't become involved in this mystery, I might never have met several wonderful people—and their names aren't Topham!"

Abby Rowen laughed aloud—the first time Nancy had heard her do this. She laughed again just as the neighbor returned. Mrs. Jones, amazed, had no chance to exclaim over the elderly woman's high spirits. Abby launched into an account of her inheritance.

As soon as Mrs. Rowen finished the story, Nancy said good-by and left. She now headed straight for the Hoover farm. The two sisters were working in a flower bed.

"Hi!" Nancy called.

"Hi, yourself. How's everything?" Allison asked, as she brushed some dirt off her hands and came forward with Grace.

"Hurry and change your clothes," Nancy said. "I have a surprise for you."

"You mean we're going somewhere?" Grace inquired.

"That's right. To Signor Mascagni's so Allison can sign up for lessons."

"Oh, Nancy, you mean—?"

"Yes. The inheritance is yours!"

"I can't believe it! I can't believe it!" Allison cried out ecstatically. She grabbed the other two girls and whirled them around.

"It's simply marvelous," said Grace. "Marvelous. Oh, Nancy, you and Mr. Crowley are just the dearest friends we've ever had." Then, seeing Nancy's deep blush, she added, "Come on, Allison. Let's get dressed."

Nancy waited in the garden. Fifteen minutes later the sisters were ready to leave for River Heights. "But before we go," said Grace, "Allison and I want to give you something—it's sort of a reward."

"Something very special," her sister broke in.

"Oh, I don't want any reward," Nancy objected quickly.

"Please take this one," Allison spoke up.

She led the way to the living-room mantel. There stood the Crowley clock. "We received it this morning from the Tophams," Grace explained.

Allison added, "We think you earned this heirloom, Nancy, and somehow Grace and I feel Mr. Crowley would want you to have it."

"Why, thank you," said Nancy.

She was thrilled, and gazed meditatively at the old clock. Though quaint, it was not handsome, she thought. But for her it certainly held a special significance. She was too modest to explain to Allison and Grace why she would prize the heirloom, and besides, her feeling was something she could not put into words. Actually she had become attached to the clock because of its association with her recent adventure.

"This is the first mystery I've solved alone," she thought. "I wonder if I'll ever have another one half so thrilling."

As Nancy stood looking wistfully at the old clock she little dreamed that in the near future she would be involved in *The Hidden Staircase* mystery, a far more baffling case than the one she had just solved. But somehow, as Nancy gazed at the timepiece, she sensed that exciting days were soon to come.

Nancy ceased daydreaming as the clock was handed to her and looked at the Hoover girls. "I'll always prize this clock as a trophy of my first venture as a detective," she said with a broad smile.

Match Wits with Super Sleuth Nancy Drew!

Collect the Original
Nancy Drew Mystery Stories®
by Carolyn Keene

Available in Hardcover!

Celebrate 60 Years with the World's Best Detective!